Waking Up in Graceland

An Elvis Story

Kelly Peach

To Bonnie,
peace, love, elvis
and all good things!

Kelly
2015

This is a work of fiction. Names, characters, places and
incidents are either products of the author's imagination
or used fictitiously. Any resemblance to actual events, locales
or persons, living or dead, is entirely coincidental.

Comments from the advance readers:

*"Waking up in Graceland really delivers Elvis to the reader.
I felt like I was there with him in his living room."*
– Kati Eddinger, Aurora, Illinois

"I love the book. My #1 comment is I want a sequel."
– Becky Reichardt, St. Louis, Missouri

*"A dream come true for anyone who fantasizes about hanging out
with his or her favorite celebrity."*
– Chris Scherting, St. Louis, Missouri

"I loved Maggie. I felt like I was there, like it really happened."
– Cindy Denner, Lakeland, Florida

*"I adore the book. I learned a lot of interesting things about Elvis
and the story left me with a smile on my face."*
– Katie Robinson, St. Louis, Missouri

FOR ELVIS,
my inspiration

FOR MY PARENTS,
in appreciation

FOR FAMILY AND FRIENDS,
my celebration

PROLOGUE

Elvis is Back

On March 5, 1960, Sergeant Elvis Presley was honorably discharged from the U.S. Army at Fort Dix in New Jersey. The King of Rock 'n Roll had put his meteoric career on hold for two years to serve his country like so many young American men were called to do.

Two days and a couple of train rides later, Elvis arrived back in Memphis and his sanctuary, Graceland. The handsome soldier bore heavy grief in his heart. His precious mother, Gladys, had died and wouldn't be waiting for him with open arms. On March 8, Elvis went to Forest Hills Cemetery to see the tombstone and angel statues that had been placed at her grave.

Not much time for a King to grieve, though. There was work to be done to get his career humming again. His manager, Colonel Tom Parker, had done an impressive job of keeping Elvis top of mind during his military service, releasing songs and booking future appearances. But it was time to get his star back in the recording studio and on the Hollywood set.

Elvis spent much of the rest of 1960 recording music in Nashville and making movies in Hollywood. The album *Elvis is Back* was released in April and the movie *GI Blues* hit theaters in November.

The world didn't have to wait long to see Elvis perform on television either. In another strategic move by the Colonel,

9

Elvis taped performances in March for a Frank Sinatra special that would air in May. The King was paid an unprecedented $125,000 for his appearance on ABC's *Welcome Home Elvis* show, which included a two-song duet with Ol' Blue Eyes himself.

After a busy nine months, the King was back on top and 1960 was drawing to a close. There was no question where Elvis would spend the holidays – at Graceland. Though this would be Elvis' first Christmas without his mother, he was sure to share his favorite holiday at home with family and friends.

CHAPTER 1

Always on My Mind

I was born the day he died. August 16, 1977. Elvis Aaron Presley departed this world and I came into it. Not a fair trade for the universe, really. Welcome an ordinary girl in a Midwestern Catholic family. Say farewell to the King of Rock 'n Roll.

It must have been a day of mixed emotions for my parents, who were getting ready to meet their firstborn. While Mom was laboring away in the hospital, with Dad by her side until he felt faint and had to leave the delivery room, the news was breaking that Elvis had died at his Graceland home. I was born at 11 a.m.; Elvis was pronounced dead at 3:30 p.m. (He actually died of a heart attack in his bathroom at around 10 a.m.) My mom said she was holding me for the first time and watching the TV in her room with Dad when the world found out that they lost Elvis Presley too soon. People are born and people die, but this baby girl could never balance the scales with a life lived so large.

I'm the oldest of three. I have a younger brother, Mark, and sister, Sarah. My parents chose nice, normal names after I was born but they named me Joan Magdalene Coyle after Mom's two favorite saints. Dad says he was giving me a head start on being a good, Irish Catholic girl. When I was old enough to figure things out, I questioned them on why they named me after a 17-year old girl burned at the stake and a prostitute. Mom says they were strong, faithful women and important heroines. Dad says they had character.

With a name like Joan Magdalene and an imagination like mine, it didn't take long before I was suggesting a nickname to family and friends. Dad sort of planted a seed when he used to come into my bedroom in the morning and sing lyrics from Rod Stewart's song, "Maggie Mae." Yes, I liked Maggie much better. Simpler and more hip.

I remember my pretty kindergarten teacher who taught us colors, letters and numbers. I remember the girl who used to copy off of me and the girl who threw up into her hands. What I can't remember is the beginning of loving Elvis Presley. It was always just… there. I was forever curious and forever infatuated, perhaps because we shared a special date on the calendar.

My parents get the credit for my lifelong crush on the King. After all, they could have played classical music around the house. But they *rocked*. To the Beatles, the Rolling Stones… and Elvis. My dad owned all of Elvis' records. We listened to them on his stereo record player. I can still see the stack of vinyl 33s, watching one drop after the other. I think we could listen to half a dozen sides before having to get up and flip them over.

I was too young to realize that Dad was making a big mistake, as far as collections go, when he sold his entire Elvis Presley record collection to pay for a professional baseball fantasy camp. I mean, I'm glad he fulfilled his baseball fantasies and was awarded MVP at camp's end, but I'd give anything to be able to play those records today!

I love the Beatles, the Stones and many more like Jerry Lee Lewis, Chuck Berry and Aerosmith. But sharing your natal day with another's *fatal* day has bonded me to Elvis like no other. Not that there's never been another guy in my life… like one who's actually living. As a matter of fact, there's a guy right now.

It's sort of a professional friendship that has blossomed recently. We have undeniable chemistry and there's plenty of no-foul flirting. Now we're about to hit the road for a two-day work trip to Memphis.

I thought I heard a car door shut so I went to the window to see if my ride was here. False alarm. The sun was shining and there was not a cloud in the sky but it still looked cold. There was condensation on the windows and the sheen of frost on the glass. What should I expect? It's December 27.

I'm so glad to have the week off between Christmas and the New Year. The ad agency where I'm a writer/producer shuts down because not a lot of business gets conducted during the holidays. The hardware store, car dealer and mortgage rate commercials will resume again when we all start fresh next week in a new year. The new year, 2007, will be the 30-year anniversary of Elvis' death and my 30th birthday. It's a bit of a sickness with me, relating everything back to Elvis.

Thinking that I need to enjoy being 29 while I can, I quickened my pace around the house to get ready to leave, moving to the rhythm of the music playing on my iPod in the Bose machine. Elvis sang from "Bossa Nova Baby" in *Fun in Acapulco*.

When I was a kid, our family watched Elvis movies whenever we could. We would go to the video store and rent old movies to watch at home on our VCR. My favorite movie was *Viva Las Vegas*. My dad was in love with Ann Margaret and used to tease my mom about how she's lucky that Ann never came calling. Elvis was so good looking in that movie and the songs were great. I loved to watch Elvis and Ann dance to "C'mon Everybody" and wished over and over that I was the girl who pushed Elvis into the swimming pool when he sang "The Lady

Loves Me."

Elvis and Ann had an amazing chemistry. They were a lot alike, really. They had a pretty serious relationship, despite the fact that Elvis had already met Priscilla when he was with Ann. One of my favorite stories is one that Jerry Schilling tells about him scaring the daylights out of Ann one night when he caught her sneaking into Elvis' Beverly Hills home. Jerry, acting as security for Elvis, thought Ann was an intruder, when in fact she was a very much welcome visitor.

I went from room to room and locked all of the windows. I love my house. It's perfect for me. With two bedrooms, there's enough room for a roommate but I can afford it on my own. I filled Scatter's food and water bowls, and emptied her litter box. My silly cat, named after Elvis' chimpanzee. I put my Elvis Presley duffle bag and pink camouflage backpack near the front door and headed into the bathroom for the last-minute items to be packed.

Before I left the bathroom, I did a final check in the mirror. Nope, nothing in my teeth. God and my parents' genes blessed me with good looks. I was not a supermodel by any means, but I was tall and thin. Blue eyes. Straight, white teeth, thanks to a year and a half of braces. A small nose I've been told is cute. Dimples when I smile. Curly brown hair. Ugh! The one thing I'd trade in if I could. Women with straight hair have told me all my life how lucky I am to have curls. I hate them. They have a mind of their own! I've tried so many hairstyles, short and long. With all, my hair was the party in control. At present, I'd settled for a cut above the shoulders with bangs. It gave me a few styling options.

I'm always excited to go to Memphis but this trip is particularly thrilling because I've been planning and hoping it would happen for some time. The enticement grows with knowing that I'm going with a professional friend featuring acceptable flirtation. And of course, Elvis has something to do with it.

In my hometown of St. Louis, I have a bit of a reputation as an Elvis maniac. I own hundreds of his songs, all 31 of his movies and lots of books and documentaries. I persuade family and friends to go with me to Elvis Tribute Artist concerts. I've been interviewed on a local radio station a few times on Elvis anniversary dates, mostly because I know lots of stories and can fill up some airtime for the host. One time at a bar, someone dared me to name all 31 Elvis movies, which I did, in alphabetical order, and drank free for the rest of the night!

It took a while for my scheme to work but it's finally happening. I had an idea for an Elvis anniversary story for the *St. Louis Post-Dispatch*: local girl (me!) born the day Elvis died grows into Elvis maniac/hometown expert and takes local reporter on VIP tour of Graceland, including a sit-down interview with one of Elvis' lifelong friends, George Klein. I pitched the idea in 2004, with plenty of time for them to decide to do it for January 8, 2005, Elvis' 70th birthday. They didn't bite. They were busy with President Bush's successful re-election campaign, Boston's World Series sweep of the St. Louis Cardinals and priest sex abuse scandals.

I continued to pitch the story every few months. Then in December 2006, they called! Chris Streater called, to be exact. He said his editor assigned him to the feature story if I was still interested. So Chris and I are headed to Memphis in time for him to write a story to run on the King's 72nd birthday!

Another car door shut outside. I peeked out the front window and Chris was making his way to the house. Tall and thin, just how I like 'em. Wavy hair, darker than mine, brown eyes. Nice teeth and hands, other things I like in a man. I made one last quick sweep of the house, rubbed Scatter's head to say goodbye and met Chris at the front door.

"Good morning! Are you ready for an adventure?" I said, flashing my dimples because I already knew from our first meeting that he likes them.

"Well, I'm a little hung over but I've got a giant-size Diet Coke and will be in adventure mode soon," he replied.

"Should I ask how your spent your Friday night?"

"One of my college buddies was in town on business so I met him at the hotel and we had one too many at the bar. We lost track of time telling stories from our glory days." Chris took a sip of his caffeine cure. "You know, it's amazing what you can forget until someone who was there with you reminds you and it all comes rushing back into your brain."

"Sounds fun. I loved college. I dream about going back all the time. Sometimes, I dream I'm naked on campus but everyone else is wearing clothes. What do you think that means?" Chris was looking at me sideways. He wasn't used to the stuff that comes out of my mouth. I bent over to pick up my bags at the same time that he did and we nearly bumped heads. "Well, thank you, kind sir!"

"Your chariot awaits, my lady," he replied, motioning to his Acura in the driveway. "I already gassed it up so we're good to go."

We headed to the car and loaded in my things. "Do you mind if we use my GPS to get there?" I opened the passenger door. Chris was trying to get to the door before me but I beat him to it – independent woman 1, chivalry 0. "I mean, I'm sure we can figure it out but I get a kick out of the details like miles to go and estimated time of arrival. I always try to shave time off of their arrival time by driving over the speed limit."

"Oh! You're driving us to Memphis? 'Cause I could use a nap to cure this headache."

"Sure, I can drive if you want."

"I'm just kidding," he added. "I'll drive. And, yes, we can plug in your GPS." Chris started the engine and headed out of my neighborhood and toward the interstate. I'm ready for the 300 miles to Memphis with an adorable driver.

CHAPTER 2

See See Rider

Road trips are always better with someone along for the ride. I'm all for solo vacations and rocking out in the car, but it was nice to have someone to talk to.

We started out with small talk – what we ate for breakfast, the agenda for the day, the weather forecast for Memphis. We were interrupted periodically by the female British voice of my GPS telling us where to go.

Once we cleared our first 20 miles, Chris said, "Let's play 20 questions."

"20 questions?" I asked. "About what?"

"Could be about Elvis or something else. Maybe a way for us to get to know each other better."

"OK. Who goes first?"

"Me," he said. "I'm the reporter." I laughed.

"First question," Chris said. "What is your favorite Elvis song and why?" He reached for something, a digital recorder.

I looked at him. "You're going to record this?" I asked.

"Just the Elvis questions. I'm on assignment this weekend, remember? And you're part of the story. Plus, I'm driving. I hope you don't mind."

I couldn't argue with that. He hit record.

"I have two answers to your first question," I said. "My favorite Elvis *slow* song is 'Love Me.'"

"Sing a little of it for me," Chris said. "I don't remember that one."

I gave him an exasperated look because singing in front of someone is so personal. He returned the look then went back to staring at the road. I mustered a little courage and sang the first three lines then stopped.

"More, please."

"Chris!" I whined.

"I'm still having trouble remembering that one."

I continued with the next three lines.

"Very nice." He moved on. "What's your second answer?"

"My favorite Elvis *fast* song is a tie," I replied. Chris laughed. "Sorry! But I've never been able to decide between 'Suspicious Minds' and 'Burnin' Love.'"

"Two great selections," he added and began to sing "Burnin' Love." I joined in for a few lines until Chris stopped and said, "I don't know the next line."

I sang it for him, then he joined back in.

"Great song," he said. "We'll save 'Suspicious Minds' for later. Your turn. Ask me a question."

"Oh, I get to play, too!" I said. "Let me think. Tell me about your family."

"Well, I was born in Chicago," he began. "I was the baby. I have a big sister, Frankie, and a big brother, Michael. I had a good childhood. My parents worked hard; Dad was an architect and Mom stayed home and raised us kids. I played baseball in high school. I was also on the wrestling team."

I giggled when he said that.

"What's so funny?" Chris asked.

"The image of you rolling around on a gym floor in one of those leotards."

"Hey, I looked good."

"I'm sure you did," I added, still giggling. I stopped myself from making a *camel toe* or *moose knuckle* reference.

250 miles to Graceland...

"Moving right along," Chris said. "How many songs did Elvis record?"

"You know, I'm not a hundred percent sure," I answered. "I've seen several numbers. I think it's around 700. My goal, of course, is to own all of them. I have several hundred now. Elvis was the first person to be inducted into all three Halls of Fame: Rock & Roll, Country and Gospel. He has five songs in the Hall of Fame: 'Hound Dog,' 'Heartbreak Hotel,' 'That's All Right,' 'Suspicious Minds' and 'Don't Be Cruel.' Elvis won three Grammys for gospel songs and albums. But interestingly enough, he didn't *write* any songs. Elvis had an incredible ear for music, a knack for knowing exactly which songs he should record and how to creatively arrange them."

"My next question," I continued. "Where did you go to college?"

"I went about as far away as I could from Chicago and still pay in-state tuition." Chris replied. "Southern Illinois University in Carbondale."

"Oh, wow! You're a Saluki just like my Dad."

"You're kidding!"

"I'm not," I added. "SIU is one of my father's true passions. He still drives 100 miles each way to watch the Dawgs play football and basketball."

"I covered plenty of those games. I used to write for *The Daily Egyptian*."

"Is that how you got interested in journalism?"

"Are we moving on with our questions?" Chris asked.

"Oops! I guess we are. Your turn, then I want to hear about you and 'J' school."

"Tell me about Elvis' military service," Chris said. "Didn't his mother die while he was away?"

I nodded. "Elvis was drafted in December 1957 and began his military service in March 1958 at Fort Hood, Texas. He got his induction delayed so he could finish filming the movie *King Creole*. From the beginning, Elvis insisted on being treated like the rest. He got a crew cut but unlike the others, had his parents near him. They lived in a trailer near the base until Gladys got sick and returned to Memphis. She was just 46 when she died of hepatitis."

I paused briefly, then continued. "Elvis got leave from the Army but only after he threatened to go AWOL. He arrived in Memphis two days before his mother died on August 14. Ten days later, the Army shipped him out to Friedberg, Germany for the rest of his service. Because his father, Vernon, and grandmother, Minnie Mae, were his dependents, Elvis lived off base with them in a leased house at 14 Goethestrasse."

"That's insane that you know the address," Chris said, shaking his head.

"Call me crazy!"

I moved on to my next question: "How did you decide to get into journalism?"

He replied, "I had a paper route. But I also sold papers outside a local church on Sundays. I got pretty good tips; I guess people felt generous after attending mass. Eventually, sitting next to a stack of papers, I opened one up and started reading the articles. Sports, the front page. I became familiar with reporters' names and looked for their stories. What got me the most was the way they could bring things to life through writing. I started to think I could, too. I got good grades on my English papers so when it was time to think about where to go to college, I chose SIU-C because they had a great communications school – one of the top in the country. The students ran the local paper plus public TV and radio stations. I got a lot of hands-on experience. I'll tell you, seeing your byline for the first time is a big high."

Then Chris turned the tables. "This journalist wants to know if you can name all of Elvis' movies. You said you could in your story pitch, or was that just fiction?"

"Yes!" I exclaimed, then clarified: "I mean, yes, I can and no, it's not fiction."

"Go right ahead," he dared.

"Alpha order," I began. "*Blue Hawaii, Change of Habit, Charro, Clambake...*" I rattled off all 31 movies in short order.

"Impressive! Your turn."

I finally asked the question weighing most on my mind. "Are you interested in Elvis Presley or just covering a story?"

"Just covering a story," he answered. I must have looked offended. "No offense!" he added. "But I'm not into Elvis. I listened to hard rock growing up. I didn't listen to rock 'n roll oldies."

"As long as you understand that none of your rock bands would be possible without Elvis getting it all started. He was a white guy performing black music and the kids went nuts. He made the girls cry, for goodness sake! John Lennon said, 'Before Elvis there was nothing.'"

"You don't have to convince me. I get it," Chris conceded. "Everything has its beginnings. And don't worry. This isn't torture or anything. With the exception of my headache, I'm actually enjoying myself so far… enjoying your company."

I smiled out the window.

220 miles to Graceland…

"I still have some Elvis questions," Chris said as he checked the recorder. "Why were Elvis' movies so cheesy?"

"Not ALL of them were cheesy," I replied, indignantly. "First of all, have you even seen one?" Chris shrugged his shoulders. "Elvis showed a lot of promise with his acting in the early films, such as *Love Me Tender, Jailhouse Rock* and *King Creole*. Interesting fact about *King Creole*: the role was written for James Dean but he, of course, died an untimely death in 1955 so the role later went to Elvis. That should at least demonstrate the caliber of acting that was desired for that role. Many people thought it was Elvis' best performance."

I paused briefly. "When Elvis returned from Germany, his manager, Colonel Tom Parker, had big plans to put him back on the map and start churning out money. Elvis wanted to try more serious acting opportunities but the Colonel knew he could make money off of the love story musicals, with repeat plots involving Elvis juggling exotic careers and lots of women. It's sad that Elvis never got to do more acting but I think his movies have a certain place in history. They take us back to a time when life was simpler; they make us smile and laugh."

"That's definitely another way to look at it," Chris said, nodding.

"My question. What are your future career plans?" I asked him.

"I want to write a screenplay and have it made into a movie."

"Me, too! We have that in common."

"Cool," Chris said. "I'm reading a few books now about screen writing. It's different from writing a book. I have some ideas banging around in my head. I know I need to get started. It's just that I'm pretty brain-drained after a day at work so it's hard to gear up in the evenings. And on the weekends, it's pretty easy to get caught up in chores, hanging out with friends, you know, that kind of stuff."

"I met Ridley Pearson at a luncheon a few years ago," I recalled. "Since he's a national bestseller, I asked him for advice. He told me to get up one hour earlier each day and write one page. At the end of a year, I'd have a 365-page book. I think it's great advice but I'm not a morning person. I hit the snooze alarm as many times as I can until I absolutely have to get out of bed!"

Chris nodded in agreement. "Yeah, I need to figure out a plan to get something written besides what I'm assigned to write at work."

"My question," Chris said. "Elvis bought a lot of cars. What did he do with all of them?"

"I think Elvis was like any other guy," I replied. "Men love cars. And Elvis could afford them so he bought them. There's a great trick question about the color of the first Cadillac Elvis bought. Most people say pink because they know he had a pink Cadillac that was his mother's favorite, even though she never learned to drive. The correct answer is *blue* because Elvis bought a blue Cadillac first."

"So blue not pink," Chris interjected.

"Right. One of the Memphis Cadillac dealers said Elvis bought as many as 200 Cadillacs over time. Not just for himself – he bought cars for others. He was known for asking people what their favorite color was and then they'd get a car in that color. We're talking his parents, Priscilla, the Memphis Mafia, people who worked at Graceland, his nurses and, literally, strangers on the street. Elvis was a very generous man. Sometimes he would go to car lots in the middle of the night and walk around with a big flashlight, picking out cars."

"You hear about celebrities and all of their cars, like Jay Leno," Chris said. "It's hard to imagine what that would be like."

"Whether you have a fleet of cars or not, where do you go on vacation?" I asked him.

"Nice segue," he laughed. "I like to go camping and fishing, outdoor stuff like that so I don't travel too far from home – rivers and lakes within three or four hours driving distance. I haven't been outside the country much except for a few trips to Mexico to lie around a resort and drink all day. That's what we did for our honeymoon."

I did a double take. *He's been married?! This is new information.* Chris shrugged it off so I stuck with the travel topic. "Travel is my favorite thing in the world and it keeps me sane," I said. "When I get home from one trip, I start planning the next so I always have a getaway to look forward to. Europe is spectacular, by the way. Very eye opening. There's much more to this world than America! And they'll gladly tell you that, too – the Brits, the Irish, the Spanish, the Italians."

"You get around!" Chris remarked.

"I might get around but I haven't been on a honeymoon," I said, digging in a bit. "Anyway. I've been to about 10 countries and half of the United States."

Chris moved on. "Next question: when did Elvis buy Graceland?"

"1957. He was 22. He had a nice ranch home on Audubon Drive but his fans were becoming a nuisance in the neighborhood so Elvis gave his parents a $100,000 budget and told them to look for a farmhouse on property that would be more private for them, including his grandmother, Minnie Mae."

I paused briefly; I sounded like a know it all. "They found Graceland on Highway 51, a 10,000 square-foot mansion on 14 acres. It was built in 1939 but was empty in 1957 and needed work. Elvis made a ton of improvements, including the stone wall surrounding it, the signature musical gates, a swimming pool and patio, a racquetball court, the Jungle Room and the Meditation Garden. Today, the mansion is nearly 18,000 square feet and is listed on the National Register of Historic Places. Just this year it was named a National Historic Landmark."

"You ought to be a tour guide."

"I am." I winked. "Yours."

"Next question: they say a man is not supposed to ask a woman her age but I've never heard the reverse. How old are you, Chris?" I asked.

"I was born during the bicentennial."

"1976. Date?" I asked.

"December 3."

"You just had a birthday! Your 30th! Happy belated birthday! I'll buy you a birthday shot on Beale Street." I said excitedly. "Wow, 30. I'm right behind you. But I just turned 29 in August so I've got a little time."

"You're 29, huh?" he inquired.

"Is that one of your questions?"

"Doesn't count," Chris said. "You said your age. And I didn't break some social taboo by asking. Now respect your elders, please."

Chris continued: "What was up with the Memphis Mafia?"

"The Memphis Mafia was Elvis' posse. Like in *Entourage* on HBO," I answered. "Elvis wasn't comfortable hanging around with other celebrities. He was most relaxed when he was with his homeboys – and he was with them *all* of the time. Just ask Priscilla, who probably would have killed for some more alone time with Elvis. The Memphis Mafia consisted of friends, managers, bodyguards, hairdressers, doctors and more. Elvis chose them based on loyalty and personality. They got their nickname in Vegas in 1960 because they dressed in suits and wore dark sunglasses. Those guys loved Elvis and worked hard for him. They were paid modest salaries but they also received food, transportation and laundry – and they got to drive his cars. Because Elvis demanded that they sleep when he slept, some of the guys popped the same pills as he did."

"I need to give my posse a nickname." Chris said.

"Speaking of posses, you mentioned your *honeymoon*. You've been married before?" I asked, very curious to hear more.

"The truth, the whole truth and nothing but the truth… yes," Chris answered. "Really? Tell me more."

"There's not much to tell," he said. "It was something that moved too fast when I was younger and wasn't a forever thing. I mean, I thought it was going to be forever but we probably should have dated longer and gotten to know each other better. If we had, we may have discovered some things about each other."

"Things…" I was even more curious.

"Things like kids and wanting to have them. I thought we both did because we talked about it before we got married. We even discussed baby names. But after we'd been married for a year or so, she either changed her mind or never wanted to have kids in the first place and sort of broke that news to me." Chris paused briefly. "At the same time, she mentioned that she had fallen in love with someone else."

"Ouch."

"Very ouch," he agreed. "But you know? It's OK. I don't hate her. I kinda wish we'd never gotten married. But I'm still young enough to have kids. I mean, meet a woman, get married and have kids."

"You're right, Chris. And I'm sorry that you had to go through a divorce."

"It was pretty quick, to be honest. What I hated the most was the limbo we were in after we got separated and before we filed for divorce. I would lie awake at night thinking about her with some other dude and would get so pissed!"

"That sucks." I sympathized.

"Such is life. I hope to meet a nice girl some day and try again. I really want to be a Dad but the thought of getting married again scares the hell out of me."

I felt bad for him. "It probably won't feel like that when it's the right person."

Chris looked over at me, "I suppose you're right."

180 miles to Graceland...

Chris picked up the recorder and looked at it but didn't turn it off. "Have we hit the 20 question mark?"

"Not sure. I haven't been counting," I replied. "Did you learn enough about Elvis?"

"I've learned more than I thought I would, thanks to your great detail. But we were just talking about marriage and it reminded me that we haven't talked about Priscilla. Tell me how Elvis met her. She had to be pretty special for him to settle down and get married with all of that fame and money and women screaming and crying over him."

I sighed. "Elvis and Priscilla are quite a love story. Like you said, Elvis had his pick of women. All the time. But I believe she was his one true love. He always came home to Priscilla. The bizarre thing, though, is when they met at a party in Germany in 1959, Elvis was 24 and she was only 14. If a 24-year old guy dated a 14-year old girl today, he'd be in jail! But this was the 1950s. Elvis thought Priscilla was the most beautiful girl he'd ever seen. He wanted to mold her into the perfect woman. He won her mother and stepfather's trust; she ended up moving to Memphis to finish high school. Can you imagine? She lived with him at Graceland. They married when she was 22 and he was 32. They had Lisa Marie exactly nine months later."

That got me thinking about my next question: "So, what qualities should your ideal woman possess?"

"Let's see," Chris began. "Big tits. Nah, I'm just kidding. No I'm not. Big tits and a nice ass."

"Pig!" I slapped him on the arm. "All you men think about is sex!"

"It's not all we think of," he countered. "We also think about food."

"Satisfy your stomach, satisfy your…" I couldn't help it, I grabbed my crotch.

"Whoa, whoa, easy there!" Chris stopped me. "I'll tell you some more about my ideal woman if you promise not to go south… yet." He continued: "OK… she's pretty. She's funny. She's smart and has a career she likes. She can take care of herself but lets me take care of her, too. Her smile lights up a room. She has a lot of friends but always makes time for me."

"Sounds like a great girl," I said. "Maybe I'll get to meet her some day."

"Maybe you will," Chris said, then turned off the recorder.

After a comfortable few minutes of silence, Chris asked, "Who are you most like, your Mom or your Dad?"

"Oh," I sighed and paused for a few seconds. It was still so hard to be asked questions about Mom.

"Did I say something wrong?"

"No, no," I said. "It's just that my Mom is gone and it hurts when the subject comes up." I put my hand to my chest.

"I'm so sorry," Chris said gently. "We can finish the question thing right now."

"No, it's OK. You need to know. It's another connection I have with Elvis because he lost his mother at a young age. I had my mom for 26 years. She was the best. Really. Pretty and smart. I have her dimples."

I smiled. "She was funny and creative, always making something at the kitchen table like sewing our clothes on her sewing machine or painting scenes on wooden plaques from the photos she took. She saw beauty in everything and everyone. When she got mad at us kids for something, she would yell, but she would get over it quickly. It wasn't until I was an adult that I realized how dedicated she was. Always running us to and from school and activities, attending as many games and recitals as she could and supporting us in what we wanted to do without spoiling us too much."

I paused. Chris glanced over at me then back to the road. I took a deep breath and continued. "In October of 2003, my mom was home alone because Dad was traveling for work. My brother, Mark, was living on his own like I was and my sister, Sarah, was away at college. Our house had three levels – two floors and a finished basement. Mom was doing her usual chores that involved running up and down the steps."

I closed my eyes and continued. "It was a freak accident. She must have tripped and fallen on the stairs because she was found at the bottom of the basement steps. Her neck was broken and," I shuddered, "she had been dead for more than a day when my brother found her."

My voice broke. A sob escaped. I felt bad because I didn't want Chris to feel awkward but it still hurt *so much*.

"Oh my God!" he whispered. "That's awful!"

"I know. It was a terrible tragedy for all of us but so traumatic for my brother. My dad and my sister had tried to call her but the phone just rang and went to the answering machine. After several attempts, my dad called my brother and asked him to go over and check on my mom. I didn't know about this at the time and I could just die."

Through tears, I continued: "I could have called her to say hi or stopped by after work but I didn't because I was wrapped up in my own busy life. What if I could have found her sooner? Maybe she didn't have to die."

Chris reached over and put his hand on top of mine. "You can't blame yourself," he reassured me. "That's not fair."

I picked up my purse from the floor in front of me and searched for a tissue. My nose always runs when I cry. "I know but I do, in a way. Even though they said her death was mostly likely instant. She probably didn't lie there and suffer for long." I paused to blow my nose. "But I just can't help but wonder. I miss her so much."

I grew quiet. Chris was quiet. I put my head back on the headrest. He reached for the recorder, which he had turned off a few questions ago, thank goodness. He tucked it into a compartment in the console. I closed my eyes. I saw my beautiful mother before her untimely death. She was smiling and laughing, somewhere in heaven. Maybe even with Elvis and

Gladys. I drifted off to sleep.

140 miles to Graceland...

When my eyes fluttered open and I realized where I was, I
immediately felt embarrassed and wondered if I'd been drooling
or doing the Jello-neck head bob. The car was quiet. I soon
realized that we were at a McDonald's.

Chris was giving me a look of concern. "You must have
needed that nap because you were out for about..." He glanced
at the odometer. "Nearly 80 miles. We're under an hour to
Memphis but I gotta pee and we should probably grab some
lunch."

He grabbed the door handle to get out and looked back at
me. "Are you OK? Hey, I'm sorry you got sad about your mom.
Really. I wish I hadn't brought it up."

I smiled. "Yes, I'm fine. And I'm sorry for getting all weepy.
I'm embarrassed. But my mom's death is still very painful for
me." I paused and reached for my purse. "I'm going in with you.
Pit stops and lunch on me."

"Lunch on you is fine but I won't make a pit stop on you," he
joked.

"Gross, Chris. Get out of the car."

After we got our food order, we were back on the road for
the final stretch. I rarely eat McDonald's and had to admit it
tasted good. Without thinking, I let out a nice belch. "Oops!" I
laughed. "Excuse me."

"Good one!" Chris laughed, too. "And I have a feeling there's
no excuse for you."

I rolled my eyes at him. "How is your hangover, by the way?"

"I'm feeling much better but I think I'll need a power nap
when we check in to the hotel."

"That's a good idea because it's going to be a busy day. Until then, let's rock out." I plugged in my iPod and played DJ for the rest of the way.

55 miles to Graceland...

CHAPTER 3

Welcome to My World

My excitement always builds as I get closer to Memphis. It's a unique city, rooted in music and civil rights history. I love that it's the South with its wonderful drawl and deep-fried cooking. I love the diversity, a city with a 60 percent African-American population. But most of all, I love it for Elvis and Graceland.

As we meandered into town, staying on 55 South, I saw the sign for Elvis Presley Boulevard and started bouncing in my seat.

"You gotta go?" Chris asked.

"No, I'm just excited!"

"How many times have you been here?"

I paused to think. "I would guess about 12 times."

"Whoa!" he exclaimed. "This is more serious than I thought."

Before long, we were on the road to Graceland. "We're checking into the hotel first, right?" Chris asked.

"Sure. It will be good to unload our stuff and you can take that power nap." "Then why did you take me straight to Elvis Presley Boulevard?"

"That's where our hotel is, too."

"We're staying at Graceland?" He was puzzled.

I gave him a look. "Not unless we're with Priscilla or Lisa. No, we're staying at the Days Inn Graceland." I laughed. "But don't worry. It's a cute little place right across the street from the mansion."

"There's no escaping it."

"Ha ha," I said, sarcastically. "Now look alive… we're getting closer… up there on your left… see the gates? It's… Graceland!"

Chris slowed the car a bit as we passed. I clapped my hands and bounced some more. "Oh, it feels so good to be back! Hi, Elvis! See you soon!" I said, enthused. Chris looked amused then pointed to the airplanes across the street. "Lisa Marie and the Hound Dog – and we'll see them up close later. Now, see that Days Inn sign up there on the right? That's where we're headed."

"You weren't kidding. That's pretty close. But I wanna stay at Heartbreak Hotel."

"It's more expensive than the Days Inn," I said. "And besides, I don't really want to stay down at the end of Lonely Street." I laughed at my joke.

"You're too much," Chris said and turned into the hotel.

We parked, grabbed our bags and checked in to two rooms – Chris in Room 223 and me in Room 222. We agreed that we'd get back together in a half hour to go on our tour of Graceland.

I think the Days Inn Graceland is perfectly themed for its location. The pool is in the shape of a guitar and Elvis music plays in the lobby and courtyard. In each guest room, framed photos of Elvis decorate the walls and… wait for it… three television channels are dedicated to Elvis! The first thing I do when I get into my room is grab the remote and see what movie or concert is on. It's not like I haven't seen them all but I enjoy trying to see how fast I can guess which movie it is. Some are easier than others, especially if you know his co-stars. When a movie ends on these channels, the main screen pops up like a DVD and just sits there until the front desk changes it. Believe me, I have called them before to remind them!

I unpacked my bag, brushed my hair and teeth, and loaded up a little purse. With my remaining minutes before meeting Chris, I plopped on the king size bed and channel surfed between *Girl Happy, Spinout* and *Clambake*. I wondered if someone had requested the Shelly Fabares movies – she was in all of these and was the only one of Elvis' co-stars to appear in three of his movies.

When it was near time to meet Chris, I headed outside to the balcony to wait, even though it was cold. I started singing along to "Stop, Look and Listen" from *Spinout*; it was playing on Elvis Radio from the pool area below. A couple of minutes later, Chris walked up, looking half awake after his nap.

We headed to Graceland on foot. While the mansion is across the street, the rest of the Graceland experience is on our side of the street. All run by Elvis Presley Enterprises. We passed Elvis' car museum on the way to buy tickets, complete with a Cadillac convertible outside where people were taking photos, and a delightful series of restaurants and shops. I was itching to go inside each and every shop along the way but was not sure if I would get to do that on this trip. I was on a mission – I have to convert Chris into an Elvis fan and there's not much time! I laughed to myself.

"What are you laughing at?" he asked.

"Oh, just wondering if you'll cross over to the dark side."

"How could I not, given this Disneyesque setup?" he said with a note of sarcasm.

We arrived at the ticket offices. "Funny you should say

that about Disney," I said, preparing to download more Elvis knowledge. "I think you'll be impressed with how easily they flow people through this attraction. It's the second most visited private home in the US, you know, with 600,000 people each year. It's as organized as any Disney theme park."

"What's the most visited private home in the US?" Chris asked.

"The White House!" Chris just shook his head, amused.

We moved quickly through the line to pick up our two VIP mansion tour tickets, which would allow us access to the mansion and grounds, and all of the other displays on this side of the street – the car museum, airplanes and special exhibits. The sales associate also handed me two more media badges and told us we should show them to one of the Graceland team members when we finished our tour. We would then be escorted to a behind-the-scenes location on the property for our meeting with Elvis' friend, George Klein.

Since we had about 20 minutes until our bus time, I told Chris I wanted to hit a couple of shops. He was a good sport and followed me around while I power shopped. I picked up a trivia game and yet another pair of sunglasses – because I tend to wear them out. Next I asked the sales girl some questions about a piece of TCB jewelry that I've had my eyes on. Intrigued, Chris asked what TCB means.

"TCB stands for 'Takin' Care of Business' lightning fast," I enthusiastically explained. "Elvis and Priscilla designed this icon in 1970. Actually, Priscilla designed it on a plane from California to Memphis. Elvis had about a dozen necklaces created for the members of his Memphis Mafia. For the wives and girlfriends, they designed a TLC necklace, which stands for

Tender Loving Care. Elvis later gave them away to celebrities he would meet at concerts. One of these days I want to buy a real TCB necklace made of gold and diamonds, but for now I'm pretty happy with costume jewelry."

Just as the sales woman brought a sterling silver TCB necklace out of the locked cabinet, I noticed it was time to get in line for our bus to Graceland. "Sorry, ma'am, but I'll have to come back after our tour to make this purchase. Right now, it's mansion time!"

Like I said, Elvis Presley Enterprises has the Graceland tour well organized. When you buy your tickets, you get a bus time. While you wait for your bus, you can shop, eat or just people watch. Right before you board the bus, the staff hands you an audio tour device with headphones. Chris and I put ours on in the bus as it started to cross Elvis Presley Boulevard and into the gates of Graceland. Elvis was singing "Welcome to My World."

I've done this tour many times before so I enjoy watching other people have their experience. This time, Chris had my attention. He was ever the reporter and brought a pad of paper and pen. At one point he leaned over and said, "If I don't take many notes, may I ask the expert I'm traveling with for details?"

"Of course!" I replied. As for me, I always listen to the audio tour in hopes of hearing something that I forgot or missed.

Graceland opened for tours on June 7, 1982, five years after Elvis died. Elvis' father, Vernon, had died in 1979, making Priscilla the executor of the estate and Lisa Marie's inheritance. The money was dwindling quickly because Graceland cost $500,000 a year in taxes and upkeep. Priscilla had the idea to make money by opening up Graceland for tours.

Within one month of opening and sharing Elvis' home with his fans all over the world, Priscilla and the newly formed Elvis Presley Enterprises made all of their money back that they had invested in the project.

During the early Graceland tour years, including my first trip with my parents in 1987, Elvis' Aunt Delta was still alive and living in the house so we didn't get to see the kitchen because they were part of her living quarters. The kitchen was later added to the tour after Aunt Delta's death in 1993. I think that made such a difference because the kitchen is so memorable.

Chris and I were getting an extra treat visiting at this time of year. When you tour Graceland between Thanksgiving and Elvis' birthday in January, the grounds and home are decorated for Christmas, Elvis' favorite holiday. Even better, Graceland is accessorized with Elvis' original decorations. Blue lights that began lining the driveway in the 1960s still lead the way up the hill. On the lawn sits the King's big wooden nativity scene. The Santa, reindeer and "Merry Christmas from Elvis" displays are still in use from the first Presley Graceland Christmas in 1957. And the trees in front of the mansion are trimmed with tiny, twinkling lights.

The tour allows a glimpse of the house pretty much as it was when Elvis was alive. I made a mental note to tell Chris later how Elvis Presley Enterprises restored some of the rooms back to the way they were before Elvis' girlfriend, Linda Thompson, moved into the mansion. She was good for Elvis after his divorce from Priscilla, but I question her decorating sense. I know it was the 1970s, but from 1974 to 1977, the living room was ALL RED! Red carpet, red furniture, red curtains – with animal prints thrown in. The photos I've seen remind me of the inside of Jeannie's bottle on *I Dream of Jeannie* – too much. But Linda must have had a blast buying all of the décor and Elvis surely enjoyed making her happy.

Someone had a little sense, because they brought Elvis' original furnishings out of storage, including the coffee table, end table, lamps and a 1957 custom-made long white sofa, before Graceland opened for tours.

After our tour group entered the mansion and folks started soaking in the sights of Graceland, I admired the oil-on-photography portrait on the stairs going up from the front foyer, from Elvis' Fort Hood, Texas days. Elvis is almost blonde! That was his natural hair color. He first dyed it black for his second movie, *Loving You*. They thought it would accentuate his facial features – and they were right – he's a hunka hunka in that movie! Elvis must have liked his black hair, too, because he started dying it after the movie as well, with the exception of his Army days. Not to mention, his mama dyed her hair black.

Chris pulled off one side of his headphones to ask me if we get to go upstairs.

"No one gets to go upstairs," I whispered. "Only Priscilla, Lisa Marie and the curator."

Out of respect for Elvis, and I'm sure in reverence to the place where he died, the tours do not go upstairs. Facing the front, the King's private quarters consist of his master bedroom, bathroom and dressing room. Facing the back was Elvis' office, Priscilla's bath and dressing room and Lisa Marie's bedroom. On one of my earlier visits to Graceland, I found out that Lisa Marie's room was originally Minnie Mae's, Elvis' grandmother, until she moved into Elvis' parents' room on the first floor after Vernon married Dee and moved out of the mansion.

People either love Graceland when they see it or they hate it. I've taken both types of these folks on tours. For some, it's just too gaudy and tacky. One of my friends once said, "It looks like Elvis threw up." But you have to put into perspective the time period and the owner. Graceland is preserved from the year that Elvis died, 1977, and the King was eccentric.

Probably the most over-the-top room is the Jungle Room. Chris looked at me when he saw it and shook his head. When Elvis bought Graceland, it was a screened-in porch. In the early 1960s, Elvis converted the porch into a den lined with shag green carpet from floor to ceiling plus unusual dark wooden furniture that he bought because it reminded him of Hawaii. In 1976 and 1977, Elvis used the Jungle Room as a recording studio for his final two albums.

I was anxious to see Chris' reaction to the basement, where there's a lot to see. To the right is a poolroom with a bizarre ceiling consisting of nearly 400 yards of fabric that took three men 10 days to install. Elvis' original pool table is still there, including the corner tear from a trick shot gone wrong. Chris' eyes widened as he entered the entertainment room to the left, with bar, stereo, jukebox and three TVs. You could hear music from speakers throughout the house wired to the jukebox. Elvis installed multiple TVs after he learned President Lyndon Johnson watched all three network news shows at the same time.

While our group ogled the eccentricity in the basement, I spent a few moments staring at a simple door that is always closed – the door to Jerry Schilling's little basement apartment. When Elvis added Jerry to his staff in 1964, he gave him a tiny room in the basement that barely had space for a twin bed. But Jerry proudly considered it his own personal space inside

Graceland. It's not part of the tour but I often wonder what would happen if I turned the knob and opened the door. Would Jerry's bed still be there?

After the basement, we headed out back, beyond the carport, to Vernon's office. It's a hoot. It was even the site of a news conference on March 8, 1960, when Elvis answered media questions about his return to civilian life.

Vernon was quite a character, managing all of Elvis' finances, fan mail and personal business in his office behind the house. The Presleys grew up in poverty. I've read stories about how stingy Vernon was with a dollar. You can't blame the guy. But it had to be hilarious when his son was buying some of the most extravagant items of his time: cars, motorcycles, horses, a ranch, pickup trucks and jewelry. The list goes on.

I love the signs in Vernon's office. One on the bathroom door reads "He or she but one at the time, the boss, VEP." Another reads "Please read and observe. No loafing in office. Strictly for employees only! If you have business here, please take care of it and leave. Vernon Presley."

Chris seemed to be enjoying himself. He was listening intently to his audio tour. I paused outside Vernon's office in the yard to look at Lisa Marie's swing set. It reminds me of the one I had in the backyard where I grew up. We played on it with friends all the time. I'm sure Lisa Marie did, too. The day her daddy died, she was to have returned to Priscilla's home in California after spending her summer at Graceland.

I caught up with Chris just past Vernon's office in the smokehouse where Elvis used to shoot guns for target practice. Chris looked my way and winked. My heart thumped a little.

I smiled and admired the horses and pastures that form the backdrop of the smokehouse.

In the 1960s, Elvis bought a golden Palomino Quarter Horse named Rising Sun and put a sign on the barn that read "House of the Rising Sun." I think about Rising Sun every time I visit. I read somewhere that when the horse died in 1986, they buried him at Graceland, facing east – toward the rising run.

As we continued our tour, we visited the Trophy Room, a building full of Elvis memorabilia, including his hall of gold records, movie and wedding memorabilia, and awards. I pulled one of Chris' headphones off and whispered, "This used to be a go cart track."

In the mid 1960s, Priscilla built Elvis a go cart track on the upper patio because he liked to race so much. It included a big electric slot car track. On May 29, 1967, it was the location of Elvis and Priscilla's second wedding reception for family and friends who were not able to attend the private ceremony in Las Vegas. In the late 1960s, Elvis converted the rec room into a space for his gold records, awards and other keepsakes. He wanted to open it for tours so his fans could share in his success – kind of ironic that it's part of the tour today.

When we arrived at Elvis' swimming pool after the Trophy Room, I asked Chris, "Can you imagine the pool parties here?"

"And the girls," he replied, for which I gave him an eye roll.

We walked the short distance across the yard to the racquetball court, with another item in the lounge area that always holds my attention. It's a simple upright piano where Elvis played a couple of songs just hours before he died. He sang *Blue Eyes Crying in the Rain* and *Unchained Melody*. I try to picture what that late night/early morning must have been like. It started out as a late-night dentist appointment for Elvis, followed by racquetball with fiancée Ginger Alden, cousin Billy Smith and his wife, Jo, but ended up as a tragic day in history.

Elvis' many achievements in the music industry continue in the space that used to be the racquetball court. I closed my eyes and tried to picture the fierce physical activity and competition in 1975, when most of Elvis' friends allowed him to win to keep the peace. Now the space is brimming with more Elvis memorabilia: lots of 1970s awards and jumpsuits, along with multiple video screens so that no one can ever forget the King's dynamic performances. I pointed out RCA's wall to Chris. They displayed 110 gold and platinum albums and singles in 1992 because Elvis continued to earn awards even after his death.

The Graceland tour ends right where it should, outside in the Meditation Garden, where Elvis and his family are buried: Minnie Mae, who outlived them all from 1890-1980, Vernon, Gladys, Elvis and a grave marker for Elvis' twin, Jesse, who died at birth.

Elvis built the Meditation Garden in 1965. After his death, Vernon moved Elvis' and Gladys' graves here to give them the privacy they deserved. Each time I go on a tour, I worry about how I will feel when I get to his grave, which is surrounded by lush floral displays and an eternal flame. Rather than sadness, I'm overcome with a sense of peace. Elvis is at rest. He worked, played and loved so hard that his body could not keep up with him. He probably could have taken better care of himself but he was part of a well-oiled machine that provided for the welfare of dozens of people. Many times when Elvis needed rest, it was not an option.

His tombstone inscription written by Vernon includes these words: "God saw that he needed some rest and called him home to be with Him." *How true.*

"What did you think?" I asked Chris as we waited for a Graceland staffer to show us to where we were going to interview George Klein.

"It's a lot to take in for the first time," he replied. "First, you have this home that's lost in time. It's gaudy, it's outdated, it's much smaller than you would think, yet it's still a spectacle. Then, you learn about this incredibly talented and charismatic man who lived his life large and achieved much, all the while being beyond generous to the people he loved and strangers, too. Finally, you walk to the place where he's supposedly six feet under. On one hand, it's powerful. On the other, it's over the top."

"I'll show you over the top," I said, pointing back across the street at the airplanes. I saw a staffer heading our way with a walkie talkie. "But first, I want you to meet someone."

"Hi, I'm Jim," the staffer said. "Your timing is good. Mr. Klein has just arrived for the interview. Please follow me."

We walked behind Jim and I was giddy with anticipation. "Where are we going?" I asked.

"We're going to one of the rooms at Graceland that is not part of the tour. We share this with the media from time to time. You know, behind-the-scenes access."

"Yes, I do! Thank you very much!" I gave Chris a look to nudge him into the conversation.

"Yes," he added. "Much appreciated. It should definitely enhance the story." I hoped our escort couldn't sense his sarcasm.

Jim guided us to what was originally the garage at Graceland. In 1960, Elvis remodeled it into apartments to be used by members of his entourage. He also added an attached carport.

When we walked into the space that Vernon had remodeled after Elvis' death, I caught my breath. I had seen a few photos of this room but they paled in comparison to actually being here. I knew the space was used for special exhibits. Most prominent was Elvis' desk, a gift from RCA after *Blue Hawaii* soundtrack sales. It had a built-in radio, TV and other accessories.

"Mr. Klein will sit here," said Jim, pointing to Elvis' desk chair. "We'll bring him to you in a moment. Please take a seat here," he said, pointing to a couple of folding chairs that had obviously been brought in for this meeting.

I was all eyes, looking everywhere, soaking up everything. Elvis' books, photos and knickknacks. An organ with lots of bells and whistles. Elvis' portable phone that was surely a predecessor to the cell phone.

We didn't wait long before Jim returned with George Klein.

"This is George Klein, one of Elvis' lifelong friends," Jim said. "Mr. Klein, this is Chris Streater from the *St. Louis Post-Dispatch* and his assistant Maggie Coyle."

Assistant! What? Maybe they had to give me a title in order for me to be allowed at this meeting.

"Hello," George greeted. "I'm sorry but I've only got about 15 minutes so let's get started. I've got another appointment, something that came up last minute. What do you want to ask me?"

Chris pulled out his recorder, started it and got to work. I sat in awe of this moment.

George was a small guy, cute in his own way. Short with dark eyes and dark hair. I guessed he was about 71 years old. I couldn't help but wonder what Elvis would have looked like at

71. George was wearing a black crew neck sweater and khakis, plus a handsome gold watch. I bet the watch was the Christmas gift Elvis gave him in 1964 after they both worked ten years in show business.

"Mr. Klein," Chris began.

"You can call me George. Or GK, the nickname Elvis gave me."

"OK, George. How did you and Elvis meet?"

"I first met Elvis at Humes High School in North Memphis in 1948. We were 8th graders. Elvis had just moved to Memphis from Tupelo. We had the same music appreciation class. It wasn't long before Elvis was bringing his guitar to school and singing in front of our class."

"What was he like in high school?"

"Elvis was different than the other kids. He dressed differently – pants and jackets, no jeans. Shirt collars turned up. Colors like pink, and patterns, too. He had long hair combed back and sideburns."

"Any signs that he was going to be a big star?"

"Elvis wasn't afraid to get up in front of a crowd. And he could sing. Really sing."

"What was it like to watch Elvis perform?"

"Elvis was an incredible entertainer, the biggest talent I've ever seen. He had an… electricity. And a voice that was magical. Elvis could make you feel so many things depending on what type of song he was singing. He had the moves, too, and combined with his outrageous good looks, he was the complete package. He loved his audiences and they loved him. Elvis was the perfect performer."

"What kind of friend was he?"

"Elvis was a real friend. He was my closest friend. My best

friend." George cleared his throat and looked down at his folded hands. The room was quiet for a moment. When he looked back up, Chris continued.

"Tell me something about Elvis that people don't know or should know." George paused. I was on the edge of my seat for his answer. George began slowly. "I'm writing a book that will tell my story of Elvis. Something that can live on since I won't be around forever." George gave a half laugh. "Elvis was very smart. He may not have gone to college after high school but he had a natural intelligence. You don't hear about that much because everyone talks about Elvis as a performer, Elvis as a movie star and Elvis as larger than life. But he was also incredibly smart and I think people need to know that."

"How were you affected by Elvis' death?" Chris asked.

"It was very painful. Being Jewish, I mourned his death for a year. I said prayers for Elvis. I didn't listen to his music. My life was pretty unhappy in the years after his death. Other sad things happened, too. My mom died. I got divorced. I had some legal troubles. It took me a while to get my career back on track. For a long time, it was difficult for me to remember Elvis without getting sad."

"You mentioned your career. What have you been doing with your life since Elvis died?"

"I've devoted a lot of time to keeping his legacy alive and I've traveled the world," George replied. "I participate in Elvis events, I give speeches and I play his music. I found a new love, Dara, and got married. Beyond that, I've done voice work and DJ work. I'm on the radio, as you know."

"What's your favorite memory of Elvis?"

"Getting married in Las Vegas with Elvis as my best man," George answered definitively. "Elvis actually had something to do with me getting married. He reminded me that he was married and so were a lot of the other guys. He offered to pay for my wedding and be my best man. That was an offer I couldn't refuse. I married Barbara Little, my girlfriend of 10 years in 1970 in the International Hotel's VIP suite."

"What do you think Elvis would think of all of this?" Chris asked, motioning around the room.

"Honestly, I think he would hate it," George said emphatically. "Elvis was a very private guy. He really valued his time away from the limelight, surrounded by just family and close friends. People he could trust, people he felt comfortable around. Graceland was his sanctuary and I think he would be horrified to see it as a public space, one that is invaded by hundreds of thousands of people each year."

George paused. "I bet that's not the answer you expected. Elvis did love his fans though, so I suppose there's something good about this place that's dedicated to keeping his music and his spirit alive."

"What do you miss most about Elvis?"

"I think about him every single day. He was smart and generous and a ton of fun to be around. The best times of my life were spent with Elvis. But I think the thing I miss most is his friendship. He was a good friend and I'm very lucky to be able to say that."

George allowed Chris to take a few photos of him at Elvis' desk. I would have loved to jump in to one but didn't think that would be appropriate behavior for the reporter's *assistant*.

Jim returned to the room. "Well, I hope you got enough for your story," George said. "I'm sorry again about cutting it short but I've got to run."

As he stood up to leave the room, Chris stood too, and the men shook hands. "Thank you very much, George. A pleasure to meet you and I appreciate you sharing some of your memories and perspective on Elvis," Chris said.

"You're welcome." George shook my hand. I got a wink, too, and then he left the room. We followed Jim back to the tour bus waiting area. Our GK moment was over.

We hopped on a tour bus for the ride back across the street. I was still quivering from the rush of spending time with GK in a room most people will never see. When we got off the bus, Chris and I headed for the airplanes.

Elvis bought the Lisa Marie, his private jet, in 1975. The 1958 Delta passenger jet cost $250,000. Elvis spent $800,000 remodeling it into what he called "Flying Graceland." The plane included a sky-to-ground phone system. As a tourist, you get to walk up stairs and enter the front of the plane, then walk through it and exit the other end. I got a kick out of watching Chris' reaction to the opulent décor and furnishings. One thing that always makes me laugh – the master bed has seat belts.

"I would have liked to have flown on this bird – what a mile high club," he said with a smirk.

"You aren't kidding," I agreed.

Elvis' second, smaller plane was the Hound Dog. He also bought that in 1975 for $900,000. Its primary use was to fly his manager, Colonel Parker, around the country, so he could arrive early to the cities where Elvis would perform to get ready for the King's arrival. On this plane, tourists only get to peer inside; they can't walk through. It was decorated in very 1970s colors – bright yellows and greens.

"The Colonel had it made, " I said to Chris. "Maybe your next story can be about Andreas Cornelis van Kuijk, a smart, ruthless talent manager and illegal immigrant from the Netherlands."

"Huh?" Chris asked, stifling a yawn.

"Colonel Parker had something to hide," I teased, giving him an elbow.

We finished our interview and tours around 4pm. I was itchy to shop and guess the Chris needed a nap.

"I have an idea," I said. "How about you head back to the hotel for some chill time and I get my Elvis shopping spree on."

"Great idea. Will you be OK on your own?"

"On my own?" I laughed. "Story of my life! And yes. I'll be 'girl happy'. Not sure I can say the same for my credit card, though. Go relax. I'll text you when I get back and we'll figure out timing for dinner and Beale Street."

We parted ways.

Every time I go to Graceland, I tell myself it's probably going to be a $200 shopping expense – even though I already have so much Elvis stuff and friends buy Elvis-themed anything for me, too. But I still feel compelled to check and see if there are any new items that could be mine. I can't have my Elvis stuff end up in someone else's house, right?

I walked back to the hotel $190 later, my blue and white shopping bags brimming with new Elvis items: jewelry, shirts, books, music and DVDs. EPE, you always get me!

CHAPTER 4

Rip it Up

There's nothing like a power nap. I love doing the whole
Graceland tour but it does take a lot out of you. Even though I
had an entire king bed to myself, I awakened curled up on the
far side of the bed facing the window.

I freshened up and put on a figure-hugging red turtleneck
and jeans for dinner... for Memphis barbeque! I headed to the
hotel lobby a few minutes before our agreed-upon meeting
time. The lobby is full of Elvis décor and photos of celebrities.
I seriously doubt Willie Nelson and Wayne Newton stayed at
the Days Inn but I'm sure they admired Elvis. It's fun to look
around and listen to the Elvis music playing. Thank goodness
he recorded so many songs!

Chris strolled in to the lobby. "Now how did I, a girl, get here
before you?" I asked.

"Well, I'm sure I can get ready faster than you but Ann
Margaret was on one of the Elvis channels and she had me a
little... hypnotized."

"Aaahhh... the female Elvis! She's adorable and Elvis really
had a thing for her. Called her "Ammo." Do you know which
movie you were watching?"

"*Viva Las Vegas*," he answered.

"Very good! This is going to be easier than I thought."

"Bringing me to the King?"

"Exactly."

Chris pulled his car keys out of his pocket.

"Um… we won't need those for dinner," I told him.

"Are we walking to one of those Graceland restaurants?"

"Nope. I promised you some authentic Memphis barbeque so we're going to Marlowe's. And… they're picking us up!"

"Are you serious? What restaurant picks you up and drives you there?"

"Marlowe's does." Just as I said that, a pink Cadillac pulled up to the front doors. Chris looked at me with disbelief.

"A pink ride… how *Mary Kay*," he joked.

I hooked my arm in his to pull him forward. "Our chariot awaits, Mr. Streater." We headed to the Caddie, arm in arm.

Marlowe's is a neighborhood barbeque joint about a mile south of Graceland. When owner Tony Gigliotti bought the place in 1973, it was called the Whitehaven Ranch House. In 1982, he changed the name to Marlowe's and started serving some Italian family favorites along with barbecue. Tony made a name for himself and his restaurant by delivering his dishes to area hotels in a Pig Bus. When he retired the Pig Bus, a pink Cadillac took its place and remains a popular free shuttle service today.

The joint was hopping but we didn't have to wait long for a table. All around us were Elvis photos and memorabilia while his music played overhead. The mouth-watering smell of Memphis barbeque filled the air. My stomach growled; I had not eaten much all day.

"Are you going for the barbecue ribs or an Elvis burger?" Chris asked.

"You know, I like ribs a lot but I don't like making a mess."

The waitress stopped by and asked if we wanted to start with an appetizer. I looked at Chris, then said, "Yes, we'll have the fried green tomatoes."

"The quintessential Southern appetizer," Chris added, reading from the menu.

"Sound good?" I asked, winking.

"Well, I prefer my tomatoes to be red but I'll let you take the lead on this one."

"As it should be," I joked. "After all, you're the green one on this trip."

He nodded in agreement. "It's all new to me."

The fried green tomatoes were flavorful, with a spicy dipping sauce. Chris decided on a half slab of savory ribs with beans and cole slaw. "I hope you don't mind the mess," he said before he ordered. As for me, I did what I nearly always do when I see it on a menu – I ordered the catfish. "Catfish!" Chris exclaimed. "We're in a barbeque joint."

"I know. But I had the barbecue pork last time I was here and catfish sounds really good right now."

"It's a pretty gross bottom-dwelling fish," Chris added with a look of disgust.

"I know, but I could eat my weight of it!"

We stuffed ourselves, my corn fritters calling my name one at a time until there were none. I noticed that everything I ordered tonight was *fried*. Oh well, a special occasion. And a good base in my stomach for what was to come… a night of drinking on Beale Street!

"Man, I'm full," Chris said, rubbing his belly in the back seat of Marlowe's pink Cadillac on the way back to our hotel.

"It was so good, but I saved room for a Big Ass Beer."

"A Big Ass beer, as opposed to a Small or Medium Ass Beer?" Chris asked, then hiccupped.

"It's a Beale Street thing. Hey, should we take a cab downtown? It's just a few miles and we'll save on parking. Not to mention drinking and driving."

"Sounds like a good idea. Maybe I can expense it," Chris said with a laugh.

Our driver pulled up to the hotel doors. We tipped him and went back into the lobby and asked the front desk receptionist to call a cab for us. We took a seat to wait. "Wooden Heart" was playing from *GI Blues*. It's a different-sounding song for Elvis. I told Chris that in the movie, his character Tulsa McLean was in the Army, stationed in West Germany, thus the German lyrics in the song. Tulsa sang this song at a puppet show when the wind-up music box stopped working for the puppet master.

"Maggie, you're a little Elvis encyclopedia," Chris said. Our cab arrived. Time for Beale Street, the birthplace of the blues!

If Elvis Presley is the first thing people think of when they hear Memphis, then Beale Street is probably second. It's not big like Bourbon Street in New Orleans but it's important, with deep musical history.

I filled Chris in on some Memphis history on the cab ride – how Beale Avenue was created in 1841 and evolved into a street that was full of African American-owned clubs and restaurants, with wonderful blues musicians over the years like W.C. Handy, Louis Armstrong, B.B. King and Muddy Waters.

The nice thing about taking a cab to Beale Street is you get dropped off right at the top of this neon wonder. You can't drive on Beale Street itself; they block it off for the street crowds. Like most weekend nights, barricades direct the crowds with a line to get carded and screened by security.

Soon we were in the stream of people on Beale Street. "It's been a long time," Chris said, looking around. "And I was pretty drunk."

"So how does it look through sober eyes?"

"Well, I can read the neon signs. And they're not moving." I laughed.

We started making our way down Beale Street. The weather was chilly considering it was late December, but not so cold that we felt we had to rush to get inside somewhere. I pointed to a Big Ass Beer booth and we headed there for our first alcoholic purchases of the night. We toasted to our Elvis weekend and the drinking began.

What I love about Beale Street is how music blares out the doors of every bar. A few shops are interspersed but it's really all about the music. Chris and I gravitated toward blues music. Some bars didn't seem to mind if we walked in with our Big Ass Beers. Some preferred we drink them outside. We did a little of both, not making too much conversation, just enjoying the music and the vibe. And great people watching. Tourists are from all over the place. But the real personality comes from the musicians. They look old enough to have invented the blues. Some were brave enough to set up their instruments and speakers on the sidewalk and play in the cold. I heard W.C. Handy lyrics from his popular "Memphis Blues."

After we bar hopped all the way down Beale, Chris beckoned me into Coyote Ugly. "Let's do a shot!" he said.

"A 30th birthday shot, I owe you! And at Coyote Ugly… how convenient. I'm not getting up on the bar, OK?"

"What if I beg you to?" He pulled me by the arm. "What sounds good?"

"Well, I think a place like this calls for… Purple Hooters!" I shouted over the music.

Chris laughed. "Purple Hooters it is." He bought a couple of shots from a bartender who was bursting out of her top and shorts. It's ironic, really, that Coyote Ugly is the bar's name because it implies a guy would rather eat his arm off than wake up the ugly girl who's sleeping with him from the night before. *Drinking affects your decision-making.* I looked at Chris. He's a nice looking guy. I wondered how much better he'll start looking as the evening progresses. *Here we go*!

We got our shots, a potent mix of vodka, raspberry liqueur and white soda, and Chris turned to me. "To the story," he toasted.

"Ooh, I like that! What story?"

"The one that has yet to be told."

"To the story!" I cheered. We clinked shot glasses and slammed our Purple Hooters. We hung around the bar for a few more minutes then headed out across Beale to start conquering the other side.

By the time we got back up to the top of Beale Street, I had a nice buzz and admitted to Chris that I was cold. "Can we go into BB King's?" I asked. BB's is my favorite bar on Beale and I had saved the best for last. The atmosphere is contagious and the blues musicians on stage are incredible.

Chris asked if I want to do another shot. I passed but he did one, then ordered a couple more beers for us. We wiggled and swayed to the rhythms. On a restroom run, I put on my Elvis sunglasses. Do I look like a nerd? I don't care. I'm in Memphis! And I'm getting drunk.

The rest of the night flew by and we practically closed the place down. Chris, though intoxicated, had a good idea to leave when they announced last call so we could grab a cab while they were still available.

I collapsed into the back seat next to Chris. Close enough – and judgment impaired enough – to lay my head on his shoulder on the drive back to the hotel. Chris was humming and singing a blues tune, something about his thrill being gone. It made me giggle.

My eyes were so heavy I couldn't wait to crash in bed. Bed! I lifted my head from Chris' shoulder as a surge of panic rushed through me when I considered that Chris might attempt to get us into the same bed tonight. Even in my booze-induced, laid back state, I didn't want that to happen. That thought sobered me up a bit.

Chris paid the driver when we arrived. I wondered why it was so dark until Chris reminded me that I was still wearing my Elvis sunglasses. I put them on top of my head and we headed up the stairs to our rooms.

"Did you have a good time?" he asked.

"Yes, I had a blast."

"You're a lot of fun to be with." He ran his hand down my shoulder.

"So are you." I moved in a little closer. We were just outside my room and I knew I should be searching my purse for my room key. I shivered. "It's cold. Give me a hug." As we embraced and his aroma enfolded me, I warmed immediately, then pulled back after a few seconds. "We should keep this professional, right?"

"I guess so," he said a bit reluctantly. "Though I'd really like to kiss you." Chris leaned in and kissed me on the cheek.

"Sleep tight, Chris."

"You, too, Miss Presley." I found my room key quickly and turned to unlock the door. Once I opened it, I turned around. Chris was still pretty close. Impulsively, I reached around his neck and pulled him to me, planting a warm kiss right on his lips. "Something to dream about, handsome. Good night." I whispered in his ear.

While he looked a little dazed, I went into my room and closed the door behind me. I flopped down on the bed. *Whoa! What possessed me to do that*? Oh, yeah, alcohol. But it was kind of fun. And I kind of want some more. Does he? Is he going to knock on the door? I kicked off my shoes and fumbled with the bed covers to get under them. "Good night, Elvis. Good night, Chris." The last thoughts I had were that I was still dressed in my turtleneck and jeans and didn't brush my teeth. Lights out.

Sometime in the early morning hours, I awakened in a daze, the kind where you don't know if you're actually awake or still sleeping. Exactly how much did I drink last night? I shook my head to lose the haze but that just made me dizzy.

The next thing I noticed was the ground was *hard*. And *cold*. I blinked my eyes a few times. It was dark, but it had to be morning, right? The space around me felt smaller, more confined.

My heart started to pound more fervently in my chest. I sat up. Am I dreaming? My eyes slowly adjusted to the dark and I looked around. I was not in a bed and I was not in my hotel room! I was in the back of a small room that seemed like a storage closet. I saw some pieces of outdoor furniture. Lots of boxes stacked up. One of them was for a Christmas tree. The box had some writing on it so I inched closer to try to read it in the darkness. The letters were unmistakable: "Graceland."

Graceland?

CHAPTER 5

All Shook Up

Graceland! As in… Elvis' home? This is not right. I'm shivering.
And scared. Where is my bed? Where is my room? Where am I
and how did I get here?

I saw a door a few feet ahead of me. What's on the other side?
Do I want to know? I can't stay in this storage room forever. I
mustered the courage and worked my way through the clutter
toward the door, tripping over a coiled hose but catching myself
with a stack of milk crates weighted down by their contents.

I stood in front of the door for a few seconds before I slowly
reached for the knob. It was cold in my hands. I turned it and
the door opened toward me. That served as a bit of protection
as I hid behind it and inched my head around to see what was
waiting for me in the space beyond.

I saw an entertainment room, but not just a typical basement
hangout where parents send their teenagers. This one was
elaborate. Colorful. Several comfortable couches and chairs. A
bar area with barstools. A television, a stereo with a nice size
stack of LPs next to it. A jukebox.

Wait! I shook my head as if to knock some cobwebs loose or
wake myself up from dreaming. My sunglasses dislodged from
atop my head; I tucked into the waist of my jeans. Do I, in fact,
see a dial on the TV? I looked at the furniture and didn't see a
remote control anywhere. Records aren't that unusual; lots of

people still collect and play them. But they also have CD players or iPod stereo players. Nothing like that in this room. It's like I'm in an episode of the *Brady Bunch* or something.

I looked down at myself. I was still dressed from last night except no shoes. I suddenly remembered how the evening ended: kissing Chris at the door and passing out on the bed. I shivered and wrapped my arms around myself. What is going on? Is Chris punking me? How did he get in my room? Where did he take me? This was nerve wracking.

I touched my face. It felt the same. I ran my fingers through my hair. It was similar. Still curly and tucked behind my ears.

I felt a growing need to use the bathroom. I looked around. Would I be lucky enough to find one down here?

I found two doors facing each other and discovered they led to small bathrooms. I heard footsteps above me and my heart pounded. Who is up there? Where am I? My need to pee overrode my questions and I darted into one of the bathrooms and closed the door. The owner must be into some retro décor.

Straight to the toilet to pee. Should I flush the toilet? I dare not! Ashamed, I put the lid down and moved to the sink to wash my hands. One hand flew to my mouth to stifle my shock when I saw my face in the mirror.

It was me but with such a mess of bed head that it actually looked like a different hairstyle! My bangs were curlier. The back felt longer. I still had my natural curl but it was hanging in more of a wave and flipping up on the ends.

I rinsed my hands and reached for the hand towel to dry them. It was monogrammed with EPA. Environmental Protection Agency? The P was bigger in the middle with the E on the left and A on the right. Who is this? Something gnawed at my subconscious.

A pair of slippers on the floor rested under the towel rack. Since I was only wearing socks, I slipped my feet into them, feeling a little guilty for borrowing them without asking. I freshened up my face and hair as best I could without having makeup or a brush. I looked in the little closet and found a comb. That helped a bit.

Now what to do… go upstairs and announce myself? What if they think I'm a burglar? I took a deep breath, opened the bathroom door and made my way to the stairs. When I climbed to the top, I looked around and saw no one. I smelled food so I assumed I was near a kitchen and the people I heard were in there.

I went in the opposite direction of the kitchen to see what I may be able to discover about where I was. Something was strangely familiar about this house. I came around a big, carpeted staircase in the middle of a foyer and near what must be the front door. My heart pounded harder at what my mind was telling me. This looks like the entrance to Graceland! But how could it be? Surely it's just a coincidence. Someone else's home has a similar layout.

I looked to my right and to my left. Very Graceland. I must be dreaming. I'll wake up any minute so I might as well continue my walk through this Elvis-like nest. But when I encountered a beautiful master bedroom with poodle wallpaper and a framed photo on the dresser, I had to grab the doorjamb to keep from falling over. Could this be his parents' room? Gladys and Vernon and Elvis are in the photo. And I know Elvis gave her the first floor bedroom when they all moved in to Graceland. He chose to have his bedroom upstairs.

Fortified by the idea that I'm walking in a dream, I

maintained enough courage to head for the kitchen. Who knows, Elvis could be in there having breakfast!

I paused outside the kitchen to listen for a few moments. It sounded like there were at least three women. The aromas from the cooking made my stomach growl. "Miss Dodger, how hungry are you this morning?" I heard a woman ask.

"No more than usual, Alberta, I'll just have a small bowl of grits and a poached egg."

Did she just say Dodger? That's Elvis' nickname for his grandmother, Minnie Mae Presley! He gave her that nickname when he was a little boy after he threw a baseball during a temper tantrum that would have hit her had she not dodged out of its way.

My hand went to my mouth again. What is going on here? As I moved my hand to the door, my hand shook. Hesitantly, I stepped into the kitchen, the newest addition to this morning ensemble.

A cook stood over the stove. An older woman commanded the counter. And a young woman, a cute brunette, sat at the table. All seemed only a bit surprised to see me. Honestly, I was expecting more of a reaction to my intrusion. "Good morning," I said, somewhat timidly.

"Mornin'," they replied.

"What are you hungry for?" the cook asked.

"Umm... I don't think I'm hungry... yet?" There was a question in my voice.

"Suit yourself. Coffee's in the pot. Have a seat." I did as she said, comfortable at having something to do besides think about what in the world is going on.

"Patsy, how many more of these lovelies should we be

expecting this morning?" the older woman asked the younger woman, nodding in my direction.

Patsy! Could it be? It does look like her. Patsy's mother was Gladys' sister and her father was Vernon's brother, making Patsy and Elvis double first cousins.

"I think she may be the only one, Dodger. But I've been wrong before," Patsy added with a giggle. Dodger! I practically fell into my seat. Good thing I had set down my coffee first.

Dodger. Patsy. Bacon frying on the stove. Whether this is a dream or not, this is Graceland!

CHAPTER 6

Trying to Get to You

"What day is it?" I asked quietly.

"Wednesday," Dodger replied.

"And the date?"

"December 28," Dodger said, eyeing me warily.

"And… the year?" My voice sounded shaky.

"1960," Patsy said, getting up from her seat to come over to me, which simultaneously reassured me and scared me.

Dodger jumped in, "Young lady, what in tarnation is the matter with you?" She was a tough one. She turned to the cook and said, "With the hours that boy and his friends keep, it's no wonder they don't know their cabooses from a calendar."

"I'm sorry, ma'am," I said. "I'm not feeling that well this morning. I don't think I slept soundly last night and maybe I should just…" My voice trailed off. By this time, Patsy had hooked her arm into mine and started moving me away.

"That's alright, missy, Patsy will get you fixed up. And you can call me Dodger."

I think I swayed a bit because Patsy's arm moved around me and held me up. As we headed out of the kitchen, Patsy turned back to the cook and said, "Alberta, would you please make a hearty breakfast for my girl here and meet us in the dining room in about 15 minutes?" To me, she said, "We're going to get you tidied up a bit, then we'll give your brain and belly wakeup calls with a homemade Graceland breakfast!" Whispering, she said, "But first… you need to answer a few questions."

I followed Patsy through the halls to another hallway with a series of doors. Holy crap, I think this is the annex! The garage that Elvis converted to apartments for his handlers. Wasn't I just here with Chris to interview GK?

Patsy opened one of the doors and we went inside. It was a cute little space, definitely decorated by a woman. I had so many questions but remained quiet. Patsy, however, wanted to chat. She motioned for me to sit next to her on the bed.

"I'm Patsy Presley," she began. "I'm 19. From Memphis. I work for my Uncle Vernon as a secretary. I've got a place to stay here, and, of course with my parents, when I need a change of scenery. Now tell me who you are and a little about yourself."

I took a deep breath. "I'm Maggie Coyle. From St. Louis. I traveled to Memphis recently…" I trailed off for a second as I tried to think up the rest of my story because surely the truth would not make sense in this time warp context. "My dad. I mean… I came to Memphis with my dad. He's here on business and I'm a big Elvis fan so I begged him to bring me with him." I met her eyes, trying to figure out if she believed anything I was saying.

"Yes, here in Memphis we have Elvis, though not all of the time. How did you end up at Graceland this morning? It's not the strangest thing in the world to have one or more girls stay over after our parties. But I don't remember seeing you here last night."

There was a pause. I looked at Patsy and she patiently looked back at me.

"I'm sorry, Patsy, but I don't remember. Honest, I don't. It scares me that I can't recall how I got here. I was just… sort of… here. After I woke up."

She must have believed me because she looked concerned as she took my hand in hers. "Maggie, did any of those boys give you any pills? Did you take anything last night?"

"I... don't think so. I d-don-don't know," I stammered, fighting back tears. She put her arm around me.

"It's OK, Maggie. You're all right now. Maybe you'll remember some more after we get you revived. I imagine your daddy is about to have a fit so you need to give him a call real soon."

I panicked for a moment, wondering how I was going to pull that off. "Patsy, I'm old enough to take care of myself."

"You're right. But I'm sure he's wondering why you didn't return last night and it would be common courtesy to let him know where you are. But before you call him, let's get you cleaned up. You look like a beatnik – which is OK, it's a look – but it's too casual for him. He doesn't like jeans so let's dress you up some. Why don't you go into the bathroom and wash your face. I'll rummage through the dresser and closet."

I did as Patsy asked and felt a little better with a clean face. *He doesn't like jeans*. Who is she referring to? Certainly not my dad. There was only one other "he" I could think of and the hairs stood up on the back of my neck.

I found some makeup in the medicine cabinet and put my eyes, cheeks and lips back on. Patsy knocked on the door then came in with some clothing in her arms. "Try on this skirt and sweater. If they fit, I've got a pretty scarf picked out to match and I may even let you borrow my pearls." She smiled and I smiled back. "Maggie, you're a lucky girl to have those dimples." She winked and closed the door so I could get changed.

I shed my *beatnik* turtleneck and folded and placed clothes on the hamper with my sunglasses on top of the stack. As I did, I remembered how women used to get much more dressed up than we do now. That's the question: what is now? I was thankful Patsy didn't see my bra and underwear. I was sure they weren't... *in style*.

After I dressed in a soft purple, fitted long-sleeve sweater and narrow, charcoal gray knee-length skirt, I went back into the bedroom where Patsy was waiting.

"Look at you! Much better. Try on these shoes. I hope they fit." They did. "Come here. Let's accessorize and we'll do your hair."

She first put a beautiful double-strand of pearls around my neck. "Patsy, these are gorgeous! You should be wearing them."

"Not today, Maggie. Today, for some strange reason, I'm entrusting them to you." She patted my shoulders and followed the pearls with a pretty scarf that she tied in a knot around my neck. It complemented the colors of my sweater and skirt perfectly. She picked up a brush and started on my hair. "You have beautiful curls, Maggie. Any girl would kill to have these and not have to spend all that time in curlers."

I laughed. "They can have them. I'd rather have straight hair."

"I suppose we always want what we don't have."

"You're right about that."

Patsy swept up most of my hair into a ponytail but left some ringlets on each side by my ears and a few in back. It wasn't a bad job. I admired my transformation in the mirror over the dresser. "You look beautiful. And hopefully hungry."

"I'm starving," I said, with both hands on my stomach.

"That's good because you're in for a treat. Alberta is a great cook."

Alberta! Or Alberta VO5, as Elvis called her. Elvis gave everyone nicknames. I smiled to myself as I realized Alberta's nickname came from a popular vitamin-loaded hair care product created by chemist Alberto, hairdresser to the stars. Alberta was with the Presleys for several years. She was their housekeeper in the first home that Elvis bought for his parents on Audubon Drive and later lived at Graceland with the Presleys. She was the first person outside the family to receive a car as a gift from Elvis. *I can't believe I'm with these people!*

Patsy and I made our way to the dining room. An impressive eight-foot table dominated the room. I didn't dare sit in the seat at the far end. That was *his*. I stopped to admire the beautiful Christmas tree in front of the big window. Soon, Alberta came in with a plateful of sumptuous breakfast foods including bacon, scrambled eggs, potatoes and cornbread. The smell of it all put me in a trance. I ate quickly.

Alberta chuckled. "Slow down, girl, or you'll get sick. This ain't your last meal."

I stopped eating so ferociously, remembering my manners. "I'm Maggie. Maggie Coyle," I said as an introduction. "It's nice to meet you, Miss Alberta. Thank you for your hospitality."

"Well, you are mighty welcome and if you're still hungry after you finish your plate, come back into the kitchen and get yourself some more."

Patsy, who had gone into the kitchen, returned with Dodger. Elvis' grandmother sat her tall, thin frame across from me with a fresh cup of coffee. I repeated my introduction: "I'm Maggie Coyle. It's an honor to meet you, Dodger. Thank you for welcoming me into your home."

Patsy was smiling. "Maggie is from St. Louis. She's here in Memphis with her daddy who's on business."

Patsy suddenly looked alarmed. "Your daddy! You need to call him! I'll fetch a phone." She scurried out of the room.

My stomach, filling quickly with Southern sensations, churned. Dodger was eyeing me. "You tell your daddy not to worry – you just fell asleep before your curfew and you're getting a belly full of Graceland's finest before heading home."

Where exactly is home now? I started picking at my food more than eating it. Patsy returned with a phone on a long cord that must have originated in the kitchen. "Give your daddy a call. No sense him worrying himself half to death."

I stared at the phone then looked back at her and Dodger. "Hopefully he'll understand," I said nervously.

Dodger got up from her seat. "You finish your meal and call your daddy. We'll be in the kitchen." They left me alone.

Alone in the Graceland dining room. Where Elvis has his meals. Where was he now? I looked around for a clock and found one that read noon. Oh, he's asleep. Elvis is nocturnal. Up all night, sleeps during the day.

Wait a minute! I put my head in my hands. *None of this makes sense!* I just know I'm going to wake up in my hotel room any minute with one heckuva hangover from one helluva dream. I started at my plate and took a few more bites as I figured out how to call *Daddy*.

I can do this. Hopefully no one is listening on the other line. I picked up the receiver, heard a dial tone and dialed six numbers instead of seven so there would be no ringing. It was a rotary phone! A long time since I had used one of these. I waited for what I thought would be the right amount of time before it would be answered. Then I played the role: "Daddy? It's me. I'm sorry I didn't come back to the hotel last night. Everything's OK. And there's a reason, Daddy." I made sure to pause here and there to make it seem like he was talking back to me. "I know. I'm sorry. There's no excuse for making you worry like that. It's just that… I met some people and they're friends of Elvis Presley and they invited me to come with them to a party at Graceland and I just had to, Daddy! I saw Graceland! I'm still here! Some of us… um… spent the night… they have a lot of guest rooms here. And they're so nice… Patsy and Dodger and... did I meet Elvis? Why, yes! I did!" I lied.

By this time, the phone had started an annoying beeping because my call was misdialed. Despite the noise in my ear, I continued. "He's so handsome, Daddy, and funny and charming and... when will I be leaving?" What to say?

As if she was listening to our conversation, Patsy poked her head into the room and said, "Tell him you're spending the afternoon with us as long as that's OK with him. We'll get you back later tonight."

I continued: "Daddy, I know I've been gone for some time but you're busy with work and Elvis is asleep and won't awaken for a few more hours and I'd really like to thank him for his hospitality and say a proper goodbye... Daddy... please? It's Elvis Presley!" Pause. "Oh, thank you, Daddy, thank you for understanding! I love you! Yes, I will. I'll tell Elvis hello from you. Thanks again, Daddy. Very much. Goodbye." I hung up. Whew! I finished the rest of my breakfast plate and returned it to the kitchen. *I deserve an Oscar!*

CHAPTER 7

It's Now or Never

Patsy and I headed down to the basement where the others had gathered to play pool and hang out. I was absolutely enthralled by the guys in the room – I was among the Memphis Mafia! Some girls were there, too, but they weren't my priority right now.

One by one, I studied the guys, racking my photographic memory to put names with faces. Red and Sonny West the security force, George Klein and Jerry Schilling: they were the easiest to identify. Charlie Hodge – a little guy, kind of adorable. I knew he would eventually work on stage with Elvis and be with him until the end.

Every once in a while someone would call out a name and that helped me discover Elvis' cousins Gene and Billy Smith. Elvis and Gene grew up together and were close but would eventually part ways due to a misunderstanding. Though he was several years younger, Billy was Elvis' favorite. He was extremely loyal to Elvis and the two were together up until just hours before Elvis' death.

I figured out Lamar Fike when he made a wisecrack that had everyone laughing. Lamar was a funny guy who could make Elvis laugh but he could also make Elvis mad. The two fought often but got over their squabbles within a day or two.

I was most stumped by Alan Fortas and Ray Sitton. Alan was with Elvis before the Army. He handled transportation and would also manage Elvis' ranch in the late 1960s. Ray has an interesting story: he used to hang out with other fans at the gates of Graceland. One night, when he asked one of the guys if he could come up and see Elvis, the King liked him and gave him a job.

Patsy and I were sitting together on a couch. She interrupted my Memphis Mafia memory game: "You met him."

My head still spinning from the mental test, I replied, "Met who?"

"My cousin. Elvis."

"No! I didn't!"

Patsy's eyes narrowed. "But you told your Daddy you did. I thought maybe you remembered some more about last night."

It was apparent that Patsy listened to my fake phone conversation so I was thankful I had made it seem as real as possible.

"I don't remember any more, Patsy," I whispered so no one else would here. "I lied to my dad." I met her eyes. "I'm sorry I did that. But I thought it made more sense than telling him how I woke up and how confused I've been all day. Oh, Patsy, I don't know how to thank you for what you did for me today! You don't know me yet you were kind and helped me freshen up and calmed my nerves. I'm very sorry for the trouble I've put you through!" I touched her on the arm.

"Stop carrying on, Maggie," Patsy cut me off as she patted me on the back. "I keep an eye on all of the girls who come to Graceland. Good Lord, if you only knew how many that was! And they all get frazzled. But there's something about you that's different and I just can't figure it out. I like you and I think he will, too." She paused, looking me over. "We need to fix that lie you told your Daddy, Maggie," she said.

I looked down and fingered the pearls around my neck.

"Patsy, fixing the lie means…"

"Yes, Maggie! It means you're going to meet my cousin! Elvis Presley!"

With those words, my brain could take no more. I fainted right there on the couch.

I'm not sure how long I was out but when I came to, Patsy was dabbing my face with a cool cloth. She held a glass of water to my lips. "Take a couple of sips," she said.

I noticed that some members of the group in the basement were staring at me, especially the big redhead. Red West, one of Elvis' bodyguards. I took the glass from Patsy and whispered to her: "I'm fine. You just told me I was going to meet Elvis!"

"I suppose you're right. Even though he's a big rock 'n roll star, I still think of him as just my cousin. Say, do you feel like you can get up and walk? We should go outside for a little fresh air. It's not too chilly today. I can show you the beautiful grounds of Graceland."

I took a few sips of the water and got up slowly with a little help from her. I felt fine. We headed upstairs to put on coats. Once again, I was at Patsy's mercy for a wardrobe. She graciously accommodated me with a black and white houndstooth coat.

Patsy and I walked arm in arm around the Graceland property. It really was beautiful. I'd seen it for the first time in 1987 when my parents took me to Memphis and Graceland for my 10th birthday. That was 30 years after Elvis bought it for his parents in 1957 and 10 years after he died.

As we walked, Patsy and I talked and laughed about life, which was a stretch for my brain because I had to keep adjusting my thoughts and words to a time period when I wasn't even alive! I discovered, though, that you could talk about boys in any era. But I kept wondering why Patsy was paying me so much attention. She mentioned that she keeps an eye on the girls who end up at Graceland, but why? Isn't she more protective of Elvis? She said there is something different about me. Does it show that I don't really belong here?

It was mid afternoon when we came back inside. Tantalizing smells wafted from the kitchen. I noticed more people and more chatter, along with more hustle and bustle around the house. Folks were moving around like they had important tasks to complete; maids were dusting and straightening. I asked Patsy about the commotion and she simply said, "Elvis is awake." She told me that meant he would eventually be coming downstairs and we all had to be ready. I felt my knees start to quiver. *Hold it together, Maggie. Don't screw it up now. You're about to meet Elvis Presley!*

Patsy interrupted my internal pep talk. "Elvis is a hungry boy when he wakes up, so he'll come to the dining room first for his meal," she said. "He can eat a slab of bacon in one sitting. Can you smell it on the skillet?

Ray Sitton, one of the super-sized Memphis Mafia members Elvis called Chief, commented slyly, "I hope it's to his liking because if it's not, we may be in for another one of his bad moods."

I remembered that Elvis liked his bacon *burned*. He liked all of his meat burned, in fact.

"Shush your mouth, Chief," Patsy said quietly yet with authority. "He bought and paid for this house and keeps you fat and happy so he can be in any kind of mood he wants to be in." To me, Patsy whispered, "But I do hope it's a good one."

We went down to the basement to hang out with the others. Some were watching a game show, ABC's *Queen for a Day.* I have landed in a place where it's still OK to demean women, I thought. But make way for Women's Lib. These folks will have no idea what hit them when women start fighting back!

Those who were not watching the game show or playing pool were listening to music. That's where my attention gravitated. Apparently Elvis' music system was wired to speakers throughout the house. I wasn't sure sure who was playing DJ but I relished each song: "Only the Lonely" by Roy Orbison, an unforgettable voice. "Cathy's Clown" by the Everly Brothers, which reminded me that I never liked songs with other girls' names in them. When Brenda Lee sang "Sweet Nothings," I wondered if Elvis would whisper in *my* ear! I felt even more strongly that I had been born in the wrong decade. Why couldn't I have been born before the birth of rock 'n roll so I could experience it like these people did? Oh, to be alive when the world started to rock!

While the Drifters were singing "Save the Last Dance for Me," a hush swept across the room. Someone turned the volume down on the jukebox. I heard footsteps on the stairs. People were sitting up in their seats a bit. A couple of girls primped their skirts. I saw one girl actually adjust her breasts. Patsy reached over, patted my knee and gave me a wink.

And then it happened... Elvis Aaron Presley, the one and only King of Rock 'n Roll, entered the room with a confident swagger and half-grin, which turned into a wide smile as he jabbed his cousin, Gene Smith, nearest him and cracked a joke. Everyone laughed and I think I heard a collective sigh of relief.

I've read that Elvis' people were always on the edge of their seats until they learned his mood of the day. Patsy alluded to it a while ago. But here I was living in the moment! And it seemed that Elvis was in a good mood today.

The basement atmosphere lightened, someone put on "The Twist" by Chubby Checker and everyone started to relax and have some fun.

Elvis sat in the middle of the couch opposite the TV. One of the guys challenged another to a game of pocket billiards and they disappeared into the next room. So far, none of the girls had gotten up from their seats.

Not only could I not get up, I could hardly move a muscle. I tried to look and act like everyone else around me but I'm sure I was doing a terrible job of it. Patsy had turned to me and was telling me a story about a fan letter she read and replied to last week but I was not processing a single word she said. She could have been speaking another language for all I know.

To everyone else, Elvis Presley waking up and coming downstairs to join his friends was probably a daily event. But this was *my* reality: seeing him up close and in person for the first time. Where I come from, he's dead. But wherever I am now, he's alive! And oh, so handsome in person! Even more than on the movie screen. I know I forgot to breathe a couple of times because Patsy nudged me in the ribs, which made me gasp for air.

I stared at the King some more. He looked so young to me, just a couple of weeks from his 26th birthday. You could see his rebel spirit, the way he carried himself. But there was also a maturity, surely brought about by his Army experiences and the loss of his mother.

Elvis was wearing an outfit that might have looked ridiculous on anyone else, but he wore it well. He had on black pants, kind of a baggy style, and white ankle boots with a slight heel. I've heard Elvis was just under six feet tall so the boots took him over the mark. On top, he was wearing three layers – a black patterned jacket over a red and white striped shirt with the collar up, over a black undershirt.

I looked at his hands. I've adored them in videos and photos because hands are the #3 thing I look for in a guy after #1 teeth and #2 eyes. Elvis' hands were remarkable. Strong, thin, wonderfully structured with nails that were cared for and not bitten – one of my personal pet peeves. His hands moved around a lot as he did; Elvis didn't sit still for very long. Would I get to see those hands play the guitar or piano? *Sigh.*

His teeth. If I had to give them a letter grade it would be an A! When he smiles or laughs, he showcases lovely, white teeth. Not perfectly set like someone who has had braces, or fluorescent white like someone who has had them bleached, but just right.

His eyes. I've seen those mesmerizing blue eyes before in his movie close ups – they were all of that and then some. They could draw you right in! Thankfully, Elvis wasn't staring at me as I stared at him because I'm sure I looked like a drooling fool – one of those crazy, lovesick fans that Elvis knows all too well.

I have no idea how much time went by. George Klein came over and sat next to Patsy and leaned in to us. I tried to hide my shock at seeing George in his mid 20s after interviewing him yesterday as an older man.

"Patsy… Elvis wants to know who your pretty friend is," George inquired. "We don't remember seeing her here before."

I glanced over at Elvis, who seemed to be looking our way yet trying not to. *He thinks I'm pretty?*

"George, this is Maggie," Patsy began the introduction. "She's from St. Louis. She's in Memphis while her father conducts business here. I..." Patsy paused briefly, looked at me and continued. "I ran into her shopping today and we struck up a conversation. When I learned that she tagged along with her Daddy to Memphis because she's a big Elvis fan, I decided to make her day and invited her to spend the day with us." I looked at Patsy, admiring and loving her simultaneously as she fabricated the details of my adventure in Memphis. "Maggie, this is George Klein, one of Elvis' best friends. They went to high school together and George is a big time Memphis DJ now."

"Nice to meet you, George," I said, extending my hand to shake his. Oddly, the second time in as many days.

"The pleasure is all mine, Maggie," he replied and added, "Well, it may not be all mine if you would join me on the other side of the room to say hello to my friend Elvis."

When George spoke these words, my heart leapt. It felt like a train derailment going on in my chest. My heart was beating with a stumbling thump like it had lost its way.

I was about to meet Elvis Presley! I stood up, a bit shakily. I accepted George's arm and joined him on the short walk across the room to where Elvis was sitting. He looked very comfortable – self confident, a little cocky even. After all, he was not only the King of Rock 'n Roll but also the King of his castle! He had a bit of mischief in his eyes, too. As we approached, Elvis said, "GK, who's that pretty girl hanging on your arm?"

"Elvis, this is Maggie. Maggie, this is Elvis Presley."

"It's an honor to meet you, Elvis," I said. My voice sounded mousy. I paused briefly to gain some confidence. "You have a lovely home and very nice friends. Thank you for having me here today." *I sound so dumb!*

"Honey, I haven't had you yet but give me some time and maybe I will!" Elvis said. Sonny West and a couple of others nearby watching the scene laughed at his joke. I felt my cheeks heat up and go red as Robert "Red" West's hair. Where I come from, it's hard to get me to blush. Yet here I was and Elvis had me in a royal flush.

"I'm just..." *What to say?* "It's just... nice to be here. Graceland is beautiful and everyone is so nice. Especially Patsy." I motioned to her and she waved at me from across the room.

"Patsy is the best cuz in the world! I surround myself with the best," Elvis said. "Maggie, why don't you sit right here next to me and tell me what you think of Memphis so far."

I did what he said and inside my head, I heard angels. And trumpets. *Someone alert the media! I'm sitting next to Elvis Presley!*

CHAPTER 8

Wonder of You

Silence. *Or can he hear my heart pounding in my chest?* I fidgeted a bit in my seat. He wasn't fidgeting but he was in a constant state of movement – a wiggling foot, tapping fingers. Elvis was full of energy. No wonder he wowed everyone when he took the stage.

I looked at him. I felt my cheeks blush again so I looked away. I looked at him again. Oh, that beautiful face. It's heavenly in photographs but here in the flesh, I can't describe it with justice. It's better than heaven.

"What's the matter, cat got your tongue?" Elvis asked.

"No. I just need to stop thinking about the fact that I just met you and I'm sitting here with you. And…" I trailed off. He smiled that million-dollar smile.

"And what?"

"And… start a conversation."

"Sounds fun," Elvis joked. "How do you start a conversation?"

"Oh, by asking a question," I said, feeling a little embarrassed. "That's one way."

"Ask me a question."

"OK." I paused to think of one. "How tall are you?" Elvis laughed. I love the sound of his laugh. I've heard it in his concerts and documentaries. It's contagious. I laughed, too.

"Why do you want to know how tall I am?"

"Well, I'm tall for a girl at 5-foot-8 so I'm attracted to tall men."

Elvis leaned in a bit. "What height would I need to be for you to be attracted to me?" *What a flirt!*

"I would say… 5 foot 11?"

"You're not sure?"

"Elvis… I'm sorry. This is a silly conversation. I should have asked a better question. Never mind." Awkward pause.

"I'm 6-feet tall." Pointing to his shoes, "Before the boots." Another pause. "Is that tall enough?"

I smiled. "Yes, 6 foot is a great height." I looked down at my feet.

"My turn," Elvis said. "Where did those dimples come from?"

I did what I always do when people bring up my dimples – grabbed my cheeks to hide them. But it never works because it just makes me smile. "I think I got them from my mom's side of the family. Because when I was born, my mom said the first thing her mom asked was if I had dimples." I paused. "Grandma died when I was three. I only have glimpses of memories of her."

"I've got your mom to thank for those dimples. Tell her I said thanks, will ya?"

Ouch. I closed my eyes for a moment. *This is such a weird conversation. I'm ruining a once-in-a-lifetime opportunity with the King of Rock 'n Roll!* I must have looked upset because Elvis leaned a little closer and said, "Did I say something wrong?"

"No, no, Elvis. I'm sorry," I stammered. "It's just that… my mom is gone." That got him. Now *he* was fidgeting in his seat. *I'm an idiot.* "Elvis, I'm sorry. Can we start over? You know, with our conversation?" He looked back at me and our eyes met. "I'm sorry. I think I'm just nervous around you. I didn't mean to bring up something like that, Elvis. Honest."

He looked as though he believed me. "It's OK. Maybe we'll talk about our moms later... and how tall they were." That made me laugh. He laughed, too.

"Where are you from, Maggie?" Elvis asked. "You don't sound like you're from Memphis." *Think fast. Make up something he'll believe.*

"I'm from St. Louis. I'm in Memphis with my dad while he's on business." *Should I continue with Patsy's story or the truth? The truth that I haven't exactly figured out yet.* I chose the former. "I met Patsy in town this morning and she invited me here for the afternoon. She said she would introduce me to you since I'm such a big fan." Was that believable enough?

"You're not here as the guest one of these goons?" He gestured to his guy friends around the room.

"No, I'm not with anyone." I waited for his reaction. If anything, Elvis seemed curious.

"Welcome to Memphis, Maggie. And welcome to Graceland," he said with a sweeping gesture worthy of a king. I smiled. Elvis reached out and touched my left dimple with his fingertip. I blushed again. I couldn't think clearly. I saw Patsy across the room and waved to her. She winked back.

Billy, Elvis' younger cousin whom he loved like a little brother, was rounding up another group to shoot pool so Elvis excused himself, saying, "Make yourself at home. I'm going to go over there to beat some knuckleheads at pool."

NBC's *Huntley Brinkley Report* was on TV with the sound turned down low. The combination of the news show and music playing was a needed distraction from the thoughts that were swirling around in my mind. I hated lying about how I got here. I needed a little more time to get my story straight in my head.

I saw Elvis standing at the bar talking to Red West after he beat someone at billiards. There was more than one head-nod in my direction. Elvis was goofing around with his pool cue. It made me a little nervous to know they were talking about me but I was still happy in the moment. It was all so unbelievable!

I pretended to watch *The Wagon Train* on TV. Red worked his way over to Patsy and chatted with her. I saw her shrug her shoulders. When Red walked away, I couldn't resist so I went over and sat by Patsy. "OK. What does Elvis want to know?" I asked. "Sorry, my intuition tells me there is some information seeking going on."

"That's pretty perceptive of you, Maggie. You know, a man is not supposed to ask a woman's age so, of course, Elvis sent Red to ask me and I admitted I don't know."

I answered: "29. I turned 29 in August. I don't want to think about turning 30 yet. I guess that makes me the older woman!" I added. "I could be your big sister."

"Older and maybe wiser, which never hurt anyone."

"Well, just in case that new piece of information needs to be delivered to its enquirer, I'm going to go up and get a bite to eat in the kitchen," I said, standing up. "Are you hungry? Can I get you anything?"

"I'm not hungry now, Sherlock. I'll see you later."

I had a BLT in the kitchen. Bacon, in honor of the King. It was quite a beehive of activity. Cooks and maids. Hungry people coming and going. Kind of like a short-order restaurant but with a sense of family and plenty of laughs. I love the way they eat. Brownies for dessert. I'd get fat if I ate here all the time. Southern cooking is real comfort food.

When I went back downstairs, Elvis saw me coming and

patted the seat next to him. My heart flipped again! I went to sit beside him. They were watching *The Price is Right* – of all things – something I was familiar with. There was not a lot of talking; when Elvis wanted to watch TV, he wanted people to be quiet, although he gave plenty of feedback to the game show contestants.

During a commercial, Elvis leaned over to me and said, "You're 29, huh? Are you going to teach me a thing or two since you're older and smarter?"

"You know what they say about the aged," I said, growing in confidence to converse with the King.

"How would I know? I'm 25! Tell me, what do they say?"

"Respect your elders," I said and nudged him in the side with my elbow. *Where was this confidence coming from?*

Elvis laughed, stretched and put an arm around me. "Oh, you have my respect. And you also have a younger man's arm around you. Watch out, teacher." As I smiled, he pointed to the TV and said, "Dimples, the show is back on again." We watched the rest of *The Price is Right* together. I felt like a bigger winner than the contestants.

The phone rang a lot at Graceland; it was a busy place. The staff was trained to answer it and call for the appropriate person. As Elvis' business manager, Vernon received several calls. Only rarely did the staff summon Elvis – when the Colonel needed him, for example. I didn't notice the phone ringing but did hear someone yell down the basement steps: "Telephone call for Mr. Elvis."

Elvis nodded to Lamar Fike and said, "See who it is, will you? Not sure I'm in the mood to be interrupted."

Lamar went upstairs, came back down and over to Elvis. "It's

Miss Wood."

"Oh, Little? OK." He got up and went upstairs.

I wondered why he didn't take the call on the basement phone and then it hit me: Little. *Elvis' nickname for his girlfriend, Anita Wood!* I've been so wrapped up in my peculiar adventure I forgot to think about who Elvis would be dating now, other than the obvious long-distance relationship with Priscilla.

Anita was an actress and singer from Memphis, petite and beautiful. Elvis was pretty serious with her from 1957 through 1962. Oh boy. This could get interesting. Was she coming over?

I must have looked lost in thought because Red came over to where I was sitting and said, "Little is Elvis' #1 girl so I imagine you'll be sent packing pretty soon. Make way for Miss Wood." He winked and walked away. *Whoa! What did I ever do to you, Red West?*

While I worried that Elvis would soon return his attention to his girlfriend, he eventually rejoined us back downstairs. He paused to give Alan Fortas a whispered update. Alan nodded to whatever Elvis was saying to him. Elvis cocked his head in my direction and shrugged his shoulders.

I was beginning to feel uncomfortable so I stood up to head for the restroom, just to have somewhere else to go. I had to pass Elvis on my way and he touched my arm as I did.

"Where are you headed, Maggie?" he asked.

"Oh, just to powder my nose."

"Don't be long." *I wouldn't think of it.*

After Perry Como's *Kraft Music Hall* ended on TV, Charlie Hodge, an Army buddy who shared a love of music with Elvis, picked up a guitar and yelled across the room: "Hey Crazy, what do you say we wake this bunch up with some entertainment?"

Crazy was the guys' nickname for Elvis. Never shy when it came to singing and jamming, Elvis crossed the room, took the guitar and sat down to play. Gene turned off the jukebox. Charlie grabbed a second guitar and Red brought out a snare drum, which instantly reminded me of DJ Fontana, Elvis' longtime drummer. A blonde girl came up with a tambourine.

Elvis strummed and sang, "Blue Suede Shoes," which happened to be on the soundtrack of his latest movie, *GI Blues*. While it was a big hit for Elvis, the song was actually written and first recorded by Carl Perkins.

Eventually, everyone was involved in the jam session in some way, whether clapping and singing along, playing, dancing or acting goofy. Elvis unplugged! He had such an amazing voice.

Elvis played several rock 'n roll songs but gravitated toward gospel. He loved gospel music, sang it his whole life and often used it to unwind with his crew after a concert, singing until the wee hours of the morning. And here it was… 10, 11 o'clock at night. I wasn't tired. I was thoroughly enjoying myself – while trying to stay under the radar.

I caught Red West staring at me a few times. I hoped it was nothing but he *was* Elvis' security – pretty much his first bodyguard from the Humes High days. Red had saved Elvis from a few bullies who had cornered him in the bathroom to cut off his long hair. Elvis later repaid the favor with an offer of employment as a driver and security guard.

Elvis kept an eye on me, too, while jamming with his friends. Someone asked him to play something else from the *GI Blues* soundtrack. Now he looked and me and sang a few lines from

"What's She Really Like." Wouldn't you like to know!

As everyone was enjoying themselves, I noticed that Alan had dozed off during a mellow gospel medley. It was late; you couldn't blame the guy. The couches were comfortable. But apparently Elvis didn't like it because when he noticed, he stopped playing. The rest of the jammers followed suit. "Hey, Hog Ears!" Elvis yelled. "Are we keeping you awake?"

This startled Alan and he came to quickly, sitting up. "Ah, no, E," he replied, embarrassed. "Not at all."

"Wake your ass up, boy!" Elvis shouted. "You're at a free Elvis Presley concert and you damn sure better enjoy it!"

"Of course, E, of course. Sorry."

I felt kind of bad for Alan, and what a nickname from Elvis. But the room resumed to the jam session and it was forgotten. Elvis didn't seem to hold grudges.

Eventually, the jam session wound down. The Memphis Mafia started moving around in preparation for whatever was next. Lamar made a phone call and approached Elvis. "What's the story, Lamasides?" Elvis asked. Elvis liked his nicknames.

"The Memphian is clearing out the last regular moviegoers of the night," Lamar told him. "They say the place will be cleared out for us any time after 11:30 p.m. I just need to call them back with what movie you'd like to see."

Elvis, who had rejoined me on the couch, looked at me and I shrugged. I didn't think what I would want to see would matter to him and I was nervous to suggest anything anyway, lest I make a historic mistake and select a movie that had not come out yet. I've read several stories about movie nights at the Memphian, when Elvis and his pack invaded the local theater after it was closed to the public to watch pretty much whatever

Elvis wanted to watch – new releases or whatever else the theater chain had available.

"Lamasides, let's watch *Ocean's Eleven*," he said and Lamar got back on the phone. I immediately pictured George Clooney and Brad Pitt, but remembered there was an original. "Maggie, since you are unattached, will you be my date for movie night? That is, if you don't have a midnight curfew."

"Oh!" I exclaimed. "I nearly forgot! I don't have a curfew but I'm supposed to return to my dad's tonight! He's more protective of me when we're away from home." Elvis looked a little disappointed. I schemed a scenario. "I would love to be your date for the movies, Elvis. Perhaps if I give my Dad a call and say pretty please…"

Elvis reached for my arm and squeezed my wrist. "Do it."

I raced up the stairs to search for the same phone that Patsy had brought to me earlier today in the dining room. I found it in the kitchen. People were moving around the house but no one was really paying any attention to me. To be safe, though, I put on another phone call performance.

"Daddy?" I whispered. "I'm sorry to wake you. It's me. Everything's OK. I'm at Graceland with Elvis and his friends. He's so amazing!" Pause. "Why am I whispering? Because it's late and some people are sleeping. About that, Daddy. You see, Elvis rents out the Memphian Theater for himself and his friends and he wants to see a movie tonight and he wants me to be his date! Daddy, can I please stay out one more night? Pretty please?"

I paused as if he were either considering my request or lecturing me. Again, the loud beeping tones began because I had not dialed a real phone number. They hurt my ear so I pulled the receiver away from my face a bit. "Thank you,

Daddy. From the bottom of my heart. This is a once in a lifetime opportunity. I love you." Pause." "I will. I'll see you later. Good night."

I hung up the phone and turned around to head down the back stairs. Standing just a few feet away was Red West, shaking his head. "A phone call to Daddy, huh?" he asked sarcastically. "What was with the line beeping, Maggie?" He took a step closer to me.

"Red, take it easy," I countered. "I know you're protective of Elvis but there's nothing to worry about. I'm 29 years old and don't really need to ask my dad's permission to stay out late." Red eyed me warily. "Red, please," I begged. "It's OK. I don't mean anyone any harm. Especially Elvis. I'm just enjoying my time with him... and you... and the others."

Red took a step back, allowing me access to the stairs. As I passed him, he said, "I've got my eye on you, Maggie from St. Louis. Or wherever you're *really* from." I bristled at that last comment, then hurried down the stairs.

CHAPTER 9

One Night

I ran straight for Elvis, still a little jangled by Red. "Elvis! I'm good to go. I spoke to my dad and he's fine with me staying out. He says hello by the way."

Elvis smiled and said, "Hello back."

"*Ocean's Eleven* is your movie of choice?"

"Yep. It came out in August. Frank and Dean and the rest of those guys put together a big Las Vegas casino robbery. Have you seen it?"

"Yes and no." Elvis cocked his head sideways. "Never mind." Frank and Dean equal Sinatra and Martin. Are they called the Rat Pack yet in 1960? I better be careful!

"Head 'em up and move 'em out!" Elvis said to the group and everyone scurried into action, heading out the doors to the carport and the cars. There was an assortment of couples, as well as single guys and single girls. The girls seemed as giddy as me, though I imagine they would have preferred to be at Elvis' side like I was. Since Elvis had just asked me to be his date, I followed him outside and into his 1960 Lincoln Continental Mark 5, which he had ordered while still in the Army in Germany.

We created a caravan of sorts as we filed one by one down the long Graceland driveway and out the gates to the boulevard. I wiggled a bit in my seat. I'm going to movie night at the

Memphian! Billy and Jerry Schilling, the two younger guys, were in the back seat. I sat in the passenger seat next to Elvis, who was driving. He grabbed my hand and pulled me toward him. My heart skipped another beat; it was becoming a regular event now. But he returned his hand to join the other on the steering wheel once I was sitting next to him. Safety first.

When we arrived at the Memphian on South Cooper, it was pretty ritualistic how everyone followed each other into the lot and found parking spaces. Elvis had been in the lead on the way there, but a couple of the guys had pulled ahead, perhaps in a protective move, to lead him into the parking lot.

As we got out of the car, the Memphis Mafia joined us, guarding him, I'm guessing in case there were some stragglers who wanted to rush the King. But entering the movie theater was uneventful. Elvis did sign an autograph for the candy counter attendant. He was so nice to people! Plus, he was paying the staff overtime.

The attendant asked us what we wanted and we were given more than our share of popcorn, soda and candy. Elvis motioned to some of the guys to bring in the snacks. He extended his elbow to me and said, "Allow me to escort you to your seat." I took his arm, still not believing that this was happening.

We walked into the theater reserved for Elvis Presley whenever he wanted it. Elvis was very comfortable; he knew exactly where to go. I knew from what I'd read that he always sat in the same place, in the center about 12 rows back from the front. And tonight, I was his date! I couldn't help but wonder if we would do more movie watching or more... my thoughts trailed. "I hope you like your seat, Maggie," Elvis said, interrupting my sexy cinema scenario.

"It's the second best one in the house."

"What's the best seat in the house?" he asked.

"Your lap, of course!" Elvis laughed. Oh, how I loved hearing him laugh.

The projectionist started the movie. I was secretly glad that I hadn't seen it before, yet knew the plot from the 2001 blockbuster. Elvis was cute, giving me a plot summary so I would know what's going on.

We munched on popcorn, Kraft caramels and Butterfingers, and sipped on soda until we'd had our fill. When our hands were free, Elvis took mine in his. I could not concentrate on anything else. It was very romantic! I scooted a bit closer to him and felt the armrest jam into my ribs. I silently wished for modern-day movie seats where you can put up the armrest and snuggle.

Though he had seen the movie several times, Elvis enjoyed it once again. I tried to follow what was happening on the big screen but my mind continued to wander. Eventually, Elvis let go of my hand and put his arm around me. I made what could have been considered a bold move and put my hand on his leg. He flexed his leg muscle. He is *all man!*

About halfway through the movie, I heard someone snoring behind me. It was Red. Elvis started throwing pieces of popcorn at him until he woke up. Again, I felt a little sorry for Red. It *was* the middle of the night.

Turning around to watch Elvis' kernel-by-kernel wakeup call, I saw a few more yawns and tired faces. I knew some of these folks worked for Elvis and kept the same hours as he did, but I was certain there were others who had to work the next day. Before I turned back to the movie, I caught a dirty look from Red, directed not at Elvis, but at me. Our eyes met briefly. Something in his eyes made me feel that his animosity toward me was increasing.

The movie wrapped and the lights came up. People were stretching, getting up and collecting their coats. The two concession employees came down the aisles and told us not to worry about throwing away any of our trash; they would do it after we left. Still, Elvis handed them ours in an empty popcorn tub. We headed out of the theater by a side entrance.

The fleet of cars we filled made their way across town, cruising along the way, no attention given by anyone to the very late, or very early, hour. These folks are definitely living a nocturnal lifestyle, with Elvis as their Headmaster of the Night. For some reason, about a dozen vampire movies flooded my mind, but no Counts exuded sexy like the King. Not even Antonio Banderas.

Time made no difference to me tonight; I was sitting in the middle of the front seat. Elvis had put one arm around me while he held the steering wheel with the other. I leaned my head back on his arm and felt dizzy with a schoolgirl crush! The King was mostly quiet, listening to whatever was on the radio.

Billy and Jerry had joined us for the ride home. "What did you think of the movie, Maggie?" Elvis asked me.

"It was good! A great story. Suspenseful. And handsome actors."

"It's hard to compete with Frank and Dean's good looks."

"Not even close, Elvis. Not even close." He flexed his arm a couple of times as we drove closer to the mansion.

Each of our vehicles made their way into the gates of Graceland and up the dark driveway. I thought about how Elvis would install the beautiful blue lights along the driveway for future Christmases. We parked around the front of the mansion. Elvis whispered to me as Billy and Jerry got out of the car, "I want you to come upstairs with me tonight, Maggie. I'd like to get to know you a little better. But I don't want to make a scene or anything so we'll go in and gather with the group for a while. I'll eventually say good night and head to my room. You wait about ten minutes or so then say good night and make like you're headed to Patsy's room, but come upstairs instead." He reached for my chin with his hand and kissed me on the dimple. Then he winked. "Do we have a plan, Dimples?"

My heart was pounding. I swallowed and muttered, "Yes, Elvis, I like your plan."

We did as the King planned. Some of the group went to the kitchen to see what the cooks had left out for snacks. Some of the guys went to the basement and, despite some yawns, started up a game of pool. One of the girls put on Paul Anka's "Puppy Love," which seemed appropriate since Sonny was necking with some girl on the couch. Did I just say necking? I *have* gone back in time!

Everyone looked quite tired but no one made a move to go to bed because Elvis was still among them. He stood around the pool table, critiquing their game and I sat back in a chair and watched it all. *Am I ready for what may happen when I join Elvis upstairs? What if I say or do something that displeases him?* My cheeks flushed. I covered them with my hands. I must have looked worried or something because Elvis sat down next to me and whispered, "Penny for your thoughts."

I blinked slowly and gazed once more on his beautiful face. "No need to pay me," I said. Elvis laughed. I continued: "I'm just living in the moment, Elvis. Feeling it. Loving it." I slowly closed my eyes and had to disguise a yawn that followed.

"Aawww, look, now you've gone and passed that 'ole yawn on to me," Elvis said and he stood up and ever so subtly faked a yawn himself. "Guys, I think I hear the mattress calling me. Either that or it's the sheets." Billy laughed at that. "Good night, friends." He reached out to shake my hand, which make me chuckle. I shook his hand and then he left the room.

It was kind of funny what happened after Elvis went upstairs. Everyone stopped what they were doing and headed for their rooms. I think they were all waiting for permission to go to sleep! George and Jerry, who did not have bedrooms at Graceland, went out to their cars and left.

When I was about to be one of the only ones left, I excused myself and headed up to the bathroom near the kitchen. Once inside, I locked the door and counted the seconds until I could walk out and head up the stairs to Elvis Presley's private quarters. While I counted, I thought about how *no one* gets to go upstairs at Graceland. It was a private space, for Elvis, Priscilla and Lisa, and after he died, they decided to keep it that way.

After he died? What am I saying? Elvis is alive now! Am I a time traveler? I shook my head in disbelief. I thought about the very few photos and film shots of the second floor of Graceland. I recall the layout but hope I don't get lost when I go up there. Yet I suppose knowing my way around would be strange since I'm supposedly a new guest in Elvis' home.

When it seemed like about ten minutes, I opened the door and quietly made my way into the foyer and up the grand staircase. I knocked softly on Elvis' bedroom door and reached for the doorknob. I was surprised when Elvis, dressed in pajamas and a robe, flung open the door and scooped me into his arms, all in one move. He pulled me into the room and shut the door, again, another smooth move. *This guy has had some practice.*

The next thing I knew, the King of Rock 'n Roll planted a kiss right on my lips! Our first kiss. I could have fainted... but kissed him back instead. It was incredible; it was *more* than a kiss. It was like being *inside* of a kiss.

As his soft, full lips continued to surround mine, and I responded with the best kisses I could summon, Elvis was pushing me toward his oversized bed. The King was in charge! And how did I feel about that? He sat me down on the bed and as he undid the scarf around my neck, I couldn't help but smile, remembering my Mom's rule of four on the floor.

"I love those dimples," Elvis said, kissing both of them. He ran his fingers through my hair, pushing some of my curls behind my ears.

"Elvis. I'm embarrassed that I don't have anything else to wear."

He raised an eyebrow. "What do you need to wear, Maggie? It's derobing time!"

I giggled. "Well, how about getting me de robe?"

He laughed that great laugh of his. "De robe is in de bathroom!" We both laughed and kissed again. He pulled me up and pointed me toward the bathroom as he pulled down the covers and climbed into bed. "Oh, and Maggie..." He tossed my neck scarf to me, which I caught. "Leave your undies on. I'd like to see if my predictions are right." I gave him a questioning look. He answered with a wink.

I entered the bathroom and closed the door behind me. Sure enough, the King had laid out a beautiful blue robe for me. It was a woman's robe and I couldn't help but wonder who had worn it last. Or *how many* women had worn it.

I looked at myself in the mirror – my cheeks were flushed! I took off my sweater and skirt, leaving on my bra and underwear. *What did you predict, Elvis?*

I took off Patsy's pearls and put them in a safe place on the countertop. I primped my hair and makeup as best I could.

There were several toothbrushes in a toothbrush holder so I took a one out and added some toothpaste to brush my teeth. I turned around to look at the rest of the room while I brushed my teeth and then I saw it. The toilet. The floor in front of it. *Where he died.* I made an awful-sounding noise, a half gasp, half sob, which made me choke a little on the toothpaste. I heard Elvis call, "Everything alright in there?"

"I…" was all I could say. There was a thud. I had sunken down to my knees right there in that spot where he died and dropped the toothbrush. My mouth was a drooling mess. I was so overcome with emotion, my head fell down toward my lap and I fought back tears.

On August 16, 1977, Elvis could not fall asleep and went to the "library" to, well, do his business. Only it was his last trip to the bathroom because his heart gave out and he, very unfortunately, fell forward off the toilet and on to his face, dying of a heart attack.

Elvis entered the bathroom without knocking. I was still on the floor in front of the toilet, dazed. He rushed over to me. "What happened, Maggie? Did you fall?" He saw my mouth of foam and drool. "Are you sick?" He reached for a hand towel on a nearby rack.

The motion of him handing it to me snapped me out of it. But I must have looked a fright. I jumped up with the towel in my hand and ran to the sink to spit out the rest of what was in my mouth. I turned on the faucet and splashed water from my hands to my face and mouth. I wiped my face with the towel.

As soon as I could, I said, "I'm OK. I'm sorry. I just... got scared."

"Scared of what?" he asked, looking incredulous.

"I... it's... nothing. I'm OK, Elvis." I was looking in the mirror, trying to adjust my disheveled self and forget the horror of what I know that he does not.

Elvis came up behind me and put his arms around me, looking at me in the mirror. "Maggie," he said gently. "I'm not going to hurt you. You don't have anything to be afraid of, I promise." He leaned his head into mine, while pulling my robe back over the shoulder it had fallen off of.

Desperate to change the mood, I said, "Well, now that you've practically seen what's under the robe, are you going to tell me what in the world you predicted?"

He laughed. "Aahhh, yes. But the lighting in here is not right and I need to be sure. Come with me." He took me by the hand and led me toward the bedroom.

Once I was away from the bathroom, I started to feel better. Elvis is alive! Not dead, in whatever warp of time this is that we are spending together. Elvis led me to the bed and we leaned back on our elbows. He slid the robe off of my shoulder, like it had been in the bathroom. My eyes followed his hands.

"Red," he said. "Yes, Elvis. I'm wearing a red bra," I replied, my voice husky.

He had a devilish grin as he undid the belt of my robe. I

couldn't help but smile either; I knew what he was after. When he pulled my robe open and saw that my underwear was black, he raised an eyebrow and said "Black."

"Very good, Elvis!" I said with a laugh. "You know your colors!"

"And I also know that you're a rule breaker, which makes you a naughty girl." His voice was seductive.

"How do you figure? I don't wear matching underwear, so I'm not a good girl?"

"It's a theory. And theories need to be tested." He laid back on the pillows, pulling me with him.

"Do they." He kissed me passionately. All the while I was thinking, *I'm kissing the King of Rock 'n Roll! He's so sexy!* I wondered what would happen next. Should I just continue to follow his lead?

The introduction of his tongue and then mine made me dizzy! I fell back on the pillows. He touched my face with his hand and kissed my forehead, which I'm sure felt overheated. "You're beautiful," he said.

"Thanks but I can't hold a candle to you," I replied as I touched his face, his hair. I smiled.

"Dimples!" he said, lunging at me, kissing one dimple after the other, which led to another round of steamy lip locking.

At one point, I heard the crunch of paper and realized that we had been rolling around on top of a newspaper. While I was in the bathroom, Elvis had been glancing at the *Commercial Appeal.*

In a move that may have been a stall tactic as I pondered how far this mess-around was going to go, I pulled the paper out from under us and looked at it. "Well, lookie here," I said, sitting up. "It says that 'Are You Lonesome Tonight' is number one in the United States for the fourth week in a row. Congratulations, Elvis! Another big hit!" Feeling the need for some silliness, I got up off the bed but did not tie my robe. I went to the vanity and picked up a hairbrush. I turned to face the King, and using the brush as a microphone, I sang him a parody:

I'm not lonesome tonight
I don't miss you tonight
I'm not sorry we ended up here

Elvis was all smiles. He lay back on the pillows and put his hands behind his head, settling in for a little entertainment. I moved seductively toward the bed as I continued to serenade him:

Does your memory stray
To the basement earlier today
When I met you in a moment so dear

Elvis was cracking up now. "Lord have mercy, you even rhyme!" he laughed. He was amused at my goofy self. I dashed over to the door and pushed the robe off one shoulder again:

Does the girl in your bedroom seem naked and bare
Do you gaze at your doorway and picture her there

I waved from the doorway, then rushed to the bed and climbed on top of the King for the big finish. Elvis groaned playfully.

Is your back filled with pain

Shall I not climb on you again
Elvis dear, I'm not lonesome tonight!

I kissed him on the nose and flashed my dimples. Elvis was grinning from ear to ear.

"I got it." He tried to sit up but I was still straddling him. I slid off and he sat up.

"Got what?"

Elvis pointed at me. "Your nickname. It just came to me."

"Really."

Elvis continued: "Moody." He paused. "Yes. You're Maggie the Moody Girl. One minute you're happy, another you're sad or scared, then happy again. Moody shall be my little nickname for you."

I sat up. I wasn't that impressed with his choice. "Elvis, I'm not Moody! I'm just overwhelmed at meeting you, spending time with you, your friends, in your home. That's a lot for a girl to handle." I paused. "Don't call me Moody," I begged. "It makes me sound like an awful person."

"No, Moody, it doesn't. Moody is a girl who wears her heart on her sleeve, who lives in the moment and feels it. Like you said earlier."

Now that he put it that way, I didn't dislike it that much. I gave him half a smile. "Well, since this is the nickname portion of our little slumber party, I have one for you."

Elvis flashed that famous smirk, raising his upper lip. "You do, now?" he said coyly.

"Yes, I do. It just came to me. When I was getting changed in the bathroom, I noticed some of your cosmetic products, including a little, well just a little, *hair dye.*"

Elvis' eyebrows went up. "So?" he said a little defensively.

"So," I continued, "My special name for you shall be Jet. As in Jet Black." I gently pushed him back down on the bed and climbed on top of him again. "Or Jet as in climb on board this Jet and let's take off. Either way, you are now hereby Jet to me."

"And you shall forever be Moody to me," Elvis countered.

Our creative session stirred another round of sexy kisses. The robes came off. Passion was ignited. We got under the covers. Hands started to wander. His touch warmed me, yet I also shivered with goose bumps! I was still in my underwear and Elvis was still in his pajamas, which were not doing a very good job of hiding his excitement.

I loved the feel of him pressed against me. But then things began to change. The pace of his passion decelerated. Elvis' movements became slower. Was he losing interest in me? His eyes started fluttering closed. He yawned and rolled on to his back. I think this man is falling asleep!

I raised myself up on one elbow to watch him. I glanced at his nightstand and noticed a pill bottle and glass of water. *Sleeping pills!* I bet he took one when I was in the bathroom.

So this is how our little rendezvous is going to end. Oh, sweet baby. I smoothed a few hairs off his forehead and kissed him lightly on the cheek. "Good night, Elvis. Thank you for a spectacular day."

He reached for my hand and took it in his, placing them on his chest. "Stay with me." Elvis mumbled something else I could not make out and soon the King was in a peaceful slumber.

I, on the other had, was wide awake. Exhausted, yes, but alert with excitement of the unimaginable kind. He wants me to stay! I spent several minutes watching him sleep, his hand still entwined with mine atop his chest. Eventually, I wiggled my hand out of his grasp, tucked him in and got out of bed, walking around to the other side to turn off Elvis' nightstand lamp.

I retrieved my robe and put it on. I turned on the TV and sat on the edge of the big bed. It took me a minute to figure out why I wasn't getting any programming – TV networks used to sign off after Jack Paar or the late movie.

My mind was all over the place. I went back to the bathroom and finished brushing my teeth since I never really completed that task. I looked through some of the drawers and found a nightgown and put it on, wondering again which girl wore this before I did. But it felt good to get out of my bra and underwear, which I decided to hand wash since I literally did not have another pair.

I hung up the clean, wet panties in the shower, reminding myself to fetch them before Elvis would see them. I looked around some more but this was not my favorite room, not in the least, so I went back into the bedroom where the King lay sleeping.

Watching him made me feel sleepy. How many hours had I been awake? And what's going to happen if I fall asleep? If this was just a dream, I don't want to wake up yet!

I climbed into bed. Elvis did not stir. As I started to think about what would happen tomorrow, I dozed off. Next to the King of Rock 'n Roll.

CHAPTER 10

Treat Me Nice

The brain reacts differently when you don't wake up in your normal bed. There's confusion. A flurry of first thoughts as the senses take in their surroundings. Things don't look, feel or smell the same as they usually do.

This bed is slippery. Satin sheets. Where am I? Slowly, I realized my location. I was on my back and turned my head to the left. *Good Lord on High. It's Elvis Presley!* Sound asleep next to me. What an angel. He was asleep on his side, facing me. I rolled on to my side and just stared. What a handsome man.

Several minutes rolled by as I stared at him and assessed what has happened to my life. My trip to Memphis with Chris seems like a dream. But isn't *this* the dream? Where will I wake up tomorrow? This is scary stuff!

While my head wanted to analyze the situation, my heart told me to just… be. Be in this moment. For however long it lasts.

Quietly, I slipped from the bed and headed to the bathroom. I splashed water on my face and used some mouthwash. When I returned to the bedroom, Elvis had rolled on to his back and the covers were off of his top half. I slid back under the covers and brought them up around his shoulders. He turned his head to face me and groggily said, "Mornin', Moody."

"Good morning, Jet."

He smiled. "I'm going to sleep some more," he said. "If you're not tired, make yourself at home. Robes are allowed in the kitchen and you'll love VO5's breakfast. Oh, and when you see Patsy, ask her about the surprise we have lined up for you."

"Wow. It all sounds wonderful." Yet I made no move to get up.

"Come here and let me hold you some more." I moved closer and turned my back to him so we were spooning. He nestled his face in my hair and kissed the back of my neck. A million goose bumps sprang to life. We laid there in each other's arms. Soon his breathing deepened and Elvis was back to sleep.

For a few more minutes, I remained there in his arms, listening to the sound of him breathing. *This is without a doubt the best dream I've ever had.* Thoughts swirled around in my head, one of them, a rising hunger. The last thing I ate was popcorn and candy.

I wiggled out of his arms, tucked him back in bed and wrapped myself in the robe that had spent the night on the floor.

I freshened up in the bathroom. I remembered to put on my clean underwear and that had dried hanging in the shower. I wondered if I should get dressed or do what Elvis suggested and go down to the kitchen in my nightgown and robe. Kind of embarrassing! But I know I'm not the first, or the last, woman to take the walk of shame. And what's worse – a robe or the same outfit I wore the day before?

My hunger won out and I headed downstairs in the robe. I paused for a few seconds at the bedroom door to glance at Elvis still fast asleep. Handsome prince. I resisted the urge to go kiss him on the cheek.

The scents of the Graceland kitchen pulled me toward them like little magnets. Dodger was in her usual chair. Alberta was busy cooking for the West cousins, Red and Sonny, who must have shown up just before me. We all said good morning to each other. Maybe Red and I could start over again, on the right foot.

I didn't feel too out of place in my robe; Dodger was in a housecoat. Alberta brought me a steaming cup of coffee followed by a plate of more wonderful breakfast items. I ate bacon, fried eggs and grits at the kitchen counter. Some people turn up their noses at grits but I love the texture so color me Southern.

Patsy entered the kitchen as I was finishing my breakfast. "Good morning!" we both said, in unison.

"How did you sleep?" she asked me. Eyeing my robe and leaning in closer to me, she whispered with a sly grin, "Where did you sleep?"

I smiled sheepishly. "Don't be thinking too much." I whispered back. "I was with your cousin and we had a great time but he took some pills and fell asleep like a baby. I guess I slept some, too. But it wasn't easy. Given the circumstances."

"Yes, the circumstances. But hang around here long enough and you'll learn to sleep when Elvis sleeps – if you want to get some sleep." We each sipped our coffee. "Did Elvis tell you anything about what we planned for today?" she asked.

"Not really, but he did tell me there was a surprise."

"There is! It's a good one. We're going on a shopping spree, courtesy of my generous cousin! I was telling Elvis you showed up without a change of clothes and you'd need to get back to your daddy's and he suggested we go shopping instead. I think he's worried that your dad will not let you return to Graceland. I told him you were old enough to make your own decisions and he said, 'an older woman! I need to respect my elder and treat her well,' which led to the shopping spree idea. What do you think, Maggie?"

"I'm stunned! And excited!" I looked at my robe and my enthusiasm deflated a bit. "But I have nothing to wear!" We laughed. "Can I borrow that cute purple and grey combo you lent to me yesterday?"

"No, I want to take a *beatnik* shopping, so wear what you showed up here in."

"You would be seen in public with me dressed like that?" I said with mock surprise. We both laughed again.

"Let me get some breakfast and then we'll get ready. Let my cousin sleep. He's given us his blessing and his charge account. We are going shopping today!"

I got ready in Patsy's room. I was embarrassed to put on the turtleneck and jeans that I woke up in yesterday but didn't have much of a choice. However, it sounds like I'll have some new choices in a few hours! As I left the room, I was tempted to go upstairs and check on Elvis but didn't want to wake him. Plus, the shopping bug had bitten me. And we hoped to be back before Elvis woke up.

It was a brisk December day but the sun was shining. Reflexively, I put on my Elvis sunglasses. "They go with your outfit," Patsy said with a laugh as she selected one of the Lincolns in the carport to drive us to Gerber's on North Main in downtown Memphis. The department store took up an entire block, which was big for 1960.

"Gerber's," I said. "Anything to do with the baby food?"

"I don't think so but it dates back to the 1800s. The escalators at Gerber's are a bit famous. Goldsmith's department store was supposed to have the first escalators in Memphis, but Gerber's stole their thunder by installing and opening their escalators six months ahead of Goldsmith's."

"You gotta love retail competition."

As we walked from the car to the store, Patsy said, "This will be a lot easier than shopping with Elvis because no one will know who we are until we tell them to charge it to his account. They'll call out to Graceland and Vernon will give them authority to make the charge."

"What's it like… shopping with Elvis?"

"Shopping with Elvis happens in the middle of the night and the stores open up special for him. They don't mind but it's quite an event and if Elvis buys you something to wear, he expects you to try it on first and model it for him."

"Whoa, Patsy, will he make me do that when we get back?" I asked, getting nervous at the thought.

"It's possible but probably not since you're sort of staying in his room and you can give him a personal fashion show." She giggled.

"What if he doesn't like the items I bought?"

"He's been known to send them back. But don't worry too much. You're with me and I have a pretty good sense of what he likes." This was going to be interesting.

With the exception of my parents, I've never had a shopping spree financed by someone other than myself. It was exhilarating!

Patsy picked out a couple of new things for herself but mostly concentrated on me. I was shy at first, not knowing what to choose. I wasn't familiar with 1960s fashion but it was far more conservative than what I was used to. Nearly no pants and definitely no denim. They thought jeans were for farmers and poor people. *My, how times will change!*

After it was all said and done, I ended up with five new outfits plus a few extra pieces, including, thank goodness, bras and undies. I got two dresses, two skirts, two blouses, a sweater and shoes. With each item, I tried to be as colorful as possible, true to my personal style, though the fashions themselves weren't quite my style.

To feel a little normal, I snuck in a pair of cute brown pants that went with a brown and white polka dot blouse. I also bought a purse. Patsy insisted I get a new coat with matching hat and gloves since it was winter.

Vernon authorized the charge when Gerber's called him at Graceland. And we didn't have to carry any packages around because Gerber's will deliver them for free. Awesome! I will have to show Elvis how grateful I am for his generosity. I wonder what form of *payment* he will accept?

Gerber's was also known for their tea room. Patsy said it was a popular place to meet when downtown. We had a soda and light snack there and did some people watching. I was a little surprised that no one recognized Patsy Presley. Regardless, I was honored to be spending the day with Elvis' double first cousin.

Patsy and I misjudged when Elvis would wake up. When we returned to Graceland, Uncle Travis, Billy's father and Gladys' eldest brother whom Elvis had appointed as the first Graceland gate guard, waved us in. "You just missed your cousin, Patsy," Travis said. "Elvis was in the mood for some tackle football so the boys headed to the field at Guthrie Park."

"Thanks, Uncle Travis," Patsy said. "This is my new friend Maggie," she added, motioning to me.

"Pleasure to meet you Maggie. Oh, and your shopping bags

made it here before you did, Patsy. They're up at the house."

"Great. Thanks again."

Travis leaned in to my side of the car a bit. "If you ladies get a move on, I bet you can still catch most of the game." He winked.

"And we will." Patsy hit the gas and we headed up the tree-lined driveway.

Patsy and I relocated our packages from the dining room. I didn't want to assume that I would be staying in Elvis' room so we put all of our items in Patsy's room.

I quickly changed into a new navy blue skirt and white blouse with navy blue trim. We bundled up, me in my new red coat ensemble, and jumped back in Patsy's car for a drive to the park to watch some football.

Despite the cold, a small crowd of onlookers had gathered around the field. Elvis, looking casual in a sweatshirt, rolled up pants and tennis shoes, was the quarterback, calling the plays for his team.

As I watched him throw a pass to Jerry, I remembered that this was how the two of them had met. Back in 1954, when Elvis was a 19-year-old truck driver for an electric company and Jerry was a 12-year-old Catholic school student, Jerry was tapped by Red to be the sixth guy in a three-on-three summer football game. Jerry made a great catch from quarterback Elvis early in the game and thus his adventure with the King had begun.

The guys played a six-man game this time, too. Elvis threw several impressive bullet passes. Jerry received many of them, as he had been doing for several years. Red was an excellent, natural athlete. He was a year younger that Elvis in high school and played football for the Humes Tigers.

It was hard, serious play with these guys – lots of blocking, tackling and falling. Not a lot of laughter. Unless, of course, someone got knocked on his ass or caught one of Elvis' great passes. Those resulted in some smiles and laughter.

I was cold but it was fun watching them. Watching *him*. Knowing I was in his bed last night. Wondering if I would be there again tonight. At least I had some new clothes to wear! Or take off. Hmmm.

After the game, we piled into several cars for the ride back to Graceland. I went back with Patsy; Elvis was hanging with the guys. When I passed him, he whispered, "Nice coat, Moody."

I grinned back at him. "Thank you, Jet!"

CHAPTER 11

Don't Be Cruel

When we returned to Graceland for the second time that day, Red was down by the front gate talking to Uncle Travis. My focus was drawn to the fans outside the gate. Young people, mostly girls, congregated there in hopes of catching a glimpse of Elvis. I'm sure they dreamed of a hello, a photo opportunity or an autograph from their idol. I felt lucky to be one of the ones allowed inside. I got some looks from a few of the girls. They were probably a bit jealous. I couldn't blame them.

Patsy braked near Red and Uncle Travis to say hello. I smiled at them, still hopeful that Red and I could wipe the slate clean.

"Travis was just telling me that Elvis pulled another generous stunt today," Red said.

"Yes he did, a little shopping spree," Patsy said. "It was fun!"

Eyeing me suspiciously, Red added, "I sure hope you two kept to a budget and didn't take advantage of his good nature."

"Of course, Red!" Patsy exclaimed. "What's gotten into you?"

"Nothing. I was just talking to Travis about Maggie here and he doesn't remember her among the girls he allowed into Graceland the night before last. You know Travis never forgets a pretty girl." Travis nodded in agreement. I felt my cheeks grow warm.

"Red, you know as well as I do that there's a steady train of girls in and out of here," Patsy said. "No one expects Travis to remember all of them. And besides, Maggie is my friend, too. There's nothing to fret about, OK? Enjoy the rest of your afternoon, gentlemen!" She continued up the tree-lined driveway.

"Thanks, Patsy," I said, relieved that conversation was over. "Red doesn't like me at all. He hasn't said a kind word or given a favorable glance since I got here and I don't know why. I know I'm a stranger and he's a bodyguard, but…"

"That's just Red being protective of Elvis. He's been doing it for a long time, since their high school days. Don't give it another thought." What Patsy said made sense but still I found it difficult to keep from worrying.

Near the front of the house, the guys were setting up some boards and other items. "What are they up to?" I asked Patsy.

She looked around as she got out of her car and said, "I think we are about to see a karate demonstration."

I was cold. "I was hoping for a chance to warm up inside!"

Patsy offered me her arm and I hooked mine into hers. "Body heat will have to do for now," she added. We laughed and made our way over to be spectators once again.

While in the Army in Germany, Elvis became interested in the martial arts and was trained by a German karate expert. In March 1960, after returning to the United States, he received a black belt in karate. Elvis eventually earned a 7th degree black belt in karate and an 8th degree in PaSaRyu, an American blend of karate, kung fu and tae kwon do.

I watched Elvis assume a fighting stance. *Is there anything this guy does that doesn't look sexy?*

He looked serious and focused. He had changed into a white karate uniform. His opponent, Sonny, a big guy who would work as a Hollywood stunt man, was holding a cushion in front of him. Elvis crouched down, arms and hands in a karate stance. He suddenly jumped into the air, yelled something I didn't understand and kicked his foot into the cushion. Sonny survived the attack.

Elvis remained serious and proceeded to show us more of his moves, including breaking pieces of wood. It became clear to me that one or more of these guys was going to have to learn karate, too, in order to spar with him properly. Not all of them seemed willing to do this but I noticed that Jerry was at the ready.

Even though most of us were cold in the December air, we waited through Elvis' martial arts demonstration. He has an amazing power over people. They are at his beck and call. What must it be like, to have people ready to say "how high" when you say "jump?" It's not as if Elvis is making them rich. I think it must be a profound love. And respect. Yes, Elvis' people love and respect him.

Our group eventually ended up together in the basement with Elvis, watching TV and playing music. It felt good to warm up. Elvis kept an eye on me and when our eyes met, he winked. The black velvet shirt he was wearing looked familiar to me. I have photos of it. I wanted to ask him if it was the gift from Natalie Wood that he wore for the Elvis Presley homecoming concerts in Tupelo in 1956.

Some of the guys were in a spirited billiards game. Suddenly, we heard louder than usual, rhythmic footsteps coming down the stairs. It was Charlie, marching his diminutive 5-foot 3 frame in an exaggerated way and singing "GI Blues" from the *GI Blues* soundtrack. Laughing, the rest of us joined in and sang.

Elvis threw a couch pillow at Charlie. Is *he* going to blow a fuse? I know he didn't like making his movie musicals because he wanted to do more serious acting without breaking into a song that he didn't like. I looked at him and he was smirking, but seemed OK.

"I really like *GI Blues*," I said. "A nice military-themed love story after Elvis' service in the Army."

"Tulsa McLean ranked #2 during opening week and you watch – it will be one of the highest grossing films of the year," Sonny added.

"Then there's Pacer Burton, the first ever Native American with blue eyes!" said Gene. There was laughter. They were talking about Elvis' newest movie, *Flaming Star,* released to theaters just a week ago.

"Now, now… in Elvis' defense, they fitted him for brown contacts then decided not to use them!" Red added.

Meanwhile, Elvis's smirk had faded and he started to look miffed. "I've told you all before I don't want to talk about my movies," he demanded. "We're on vacation from all of that Hollywood bullshit." That quieted the room. *Please tell me why I, of all people, had to go and break the silence?*

"Elvis?" I said. "I think your movies have purpose. They make people happy and help them forget about their worries for a while."

Uh oh. My comments did not get the response I was hoping for.

"Purpose? What would *you* know about a goddamn purpose, other than party crashing!" Elvis said, standing up, temper suddenly flaring. "I said I didn't want to talk about it. And you have no right to give your amateur opinion anyway!" Elvis' eyes were alight. I now understood why Priscilla called him Fire Eyes when he lost his temper. Elvis crossed his arms. "I think it's time for you to leave," he said. No one else moved a muscle. I saw Red out of the corner of my eye grinning like the Cheshire Cat. *Oh no. Did he say something to Elvis?*

I forced my wobbly legs to stand up. Quietly, I said, "I'm sorry. I didn't mean to upset you, Elvis. Thank you for welcoming me to your home. I'll go now." I paused and looked around at all of the faces. My cheeks were on fire. Patsy's expression was pained and she was wringing her hands but remained quiet. My heart was pounding in my throat. I didn't want to cry. "It was nice to meet all of you and I wish you many blessings."

As proudly as I could, I left the room, climbed the stairs, holding on to the handrail for dear life lest I tumble backwards and break my neck.

I made my way to the front door. I took my new coat from the coat tree. I opened the front door, stepped outside, closed the door and found myself outside the mansion in the cold. It was getting dark. *What am I going to do? It's 1960 and I don't know where to go!* I looked down the long driveway and could see Uncle Travis near the front gate and a few fans on the sidewalk outside the property.

With shaky legs, I headed down the hill. I brushed a tear from my eye before it fell on my cheeks. There was a chill in the air so I wrapped my coat tighter around me. *Where am I headed?* My feet were moving, albeit slowly. I mustered what confidence I could in this confusing time warp. *When I get to the bottom, I'll wave goodbye to Travis and walk out the gate.* I'll ignore the stares of the fans waiting for a glimpse of Elvis. I'll find myself on Highway 51 South and see where it takes me.

Another tear fell. Damn! Why didn't I keep my mouth shut? I've read stories about Elvis' dramatic mood swings and his desire to keep his business and personal affairs separate. Not to mention he thought women should keep their mouths shut. There was just something stupid inside of me that wanted him to know that his movies are relevant. *I'm a moron!*

Travis saw me approaching and stared at me strangely. Then he looked beyond me back up the hill. That's when I heard an engine behind me. It didn't sound big enough to be a car but was coming closer. I didn't dare turn around. I kept going, moving over to the side to make way.

The next thing I know, a golf cart pulls out in front of me, like it's on a mission to run me over, scaring me half to death. It's Elvis! He's smiling and laughing. "What's a Moody girl like you doing out here in the cold?" he asked. "Get in! I've got a blanket. We'll go for a ride."

I couldn't move. Or speak. "Oh, *now* the cat's got your tongue," Elvis continued. "Sure didn't a few minutes ago, did it? Come here. The fresh air will do you some good."

I climbed into the cart with him. He wrapped a blanket around me and kissed away the tear that had fallen down my cheek, then took off up the driveway.

He calls me Moody? I think I just witnessed an Elvis Presley mood swing!

I tried to return to as normal a state as I could, considering what just happened. I faked my first smile but Elvis was driving like a maniac so it was not long before I was grinning. And trying not to fall out of the golf cart! I was tremendously relieved, too. I'm *very* glad I didn't have to leave here. Everything is really confusing for me now and I think I'm safer at Graceland until I figure out... well, figure out what has happened to my reality.

Elvis had chosen a place to stop on the property other than the carport. He scooted a bit closer to me and tucked the blanket in around us. The cold did not take away from Graceland's beauty – more than a dozen acres and even more potential. I knew it had needed work when he bought the place.

Already, you could see signs of his improvements: the stone wall, the gates, the swimming pool and patio. "Graceland is wonderful, Elvis," I told him. "Congratulations on such an incredible home for you and your family."

Elvis was quiet. He remained that way for another minute or so then said, "*Satnin* didn't get to enjoy Graceland for long." Satnin. I knew this was a nickname he called his mother. It was his first Christmas season at Graceland without Gladys and he was missing her. That hit home with me. I miss my mom, too. I was unsure if I should ask who Satnin was or say anything so I remained quiet but did reach for his hand under the blanket.

"What happened to your mama, Moody?" Elvis asked.

I took a deep breath and gathered some courage. "It was a horrible accident." I closed my eyes. Elvis squeezed my hand. "She was home alone and fell down a flight of stairs and broke her neck." I lowered my head. "If only I was home when it happened. Maybe..." I put my head in my hand. "I didn't get to say goodbye. I didn't get to tell her I loved her one more time. I miss her terribly." I started to cry softly, my emotions already raw from him yelling at me. Elvis let got of my hand to put both arms around me. He held me close. I leaned into his embrace and held on to his arm.

Elvis spoke again: "I've got a funny feeling, Moody."

"What about?"

"It's been pressing on me all day. Kind of a hunch but hard to translate." He paused in thought. "It just seems to be saying 'time is short.'"

I was wracked by a sob and tried to recover it as soon as it escaped. Elvis didn't miss it. He hugged me tighter.

"Time *is* short. Life is short," I said. "It was too short for your mama. Too short for mine. Too short for us." My voice broke as I said that. I put my head on his shoulder. More tears fell. For Mom, for Gladys. For Elvis, this incredibly soulful man who just might have a sixth sense about his mortality.

"What do you mean, 'time is short for us,' Moody?" Elvis asked. "You think we're gonna die young like our mothers?"

Oh my God, where is this going? I had to recover; I couldn't take any more of this deep, emotional conversation. I wiped away my tears and turned to face him. "No, no. We're both young and vibrant and healthy so I don't think that. "What I meant was this time we have together is short. You and me. We just met yesterday. We had an incredible time. Today has been fun. Well, we went off track for just a little bit. But sooner or later, we'll both have to get back to what we were doing before we met. Back to reality. I know you have girlfriends and movies and music. And I have…" I stopped, unsure of what to say.

"You have what?" Elvis pried.

I continued: "I'm from out of town. I have a job and a paycheck to get back to at the advertising agency. My dad…"

Elvis interrupted: "Your dad! Have you talked to him since last night?"

"No, and I should probably check in. He knows I'm with you

so I don't think he's worried. Plus, I'm old enough to take care of myself."

"I thought you just said you were young and vibrant?" Elvis joked.

"Ha. Ha. You know what I mean. I did come on this business trip with him."

"Let's go see him," he suggested.

"Who? My Dad?" *Yikes!*

"Yes." Elvis turned on the golf cart and started heading back to the carport. "Let's hop in the car and head downtown so you can check in with your dad at his hotel. One condition, though."

My mind was racing. *How in the heck am I going to pull this off?*

Elvis nudged me. "Do you want to hear the condition?"

"What? Oh. Yes. What is it?"

"You tell him you want to stay for a couple more days. I've got a date for New Year's Eve but until then, this is our time. What do you say, Moody? Time is short, right?"

"Yes, Elvis. Yes, I'll stay. Time is short so let's make the most of it."

All the while I'm wondering how I'm going to make *Daddy* appear out of thin air!

Elvis opened the door of his car to let me inside. "I'm gonna run inside and tell someone where we're going. The keys are in the ignition. Fire it up and get the heater going. I'll be right back." Elvis closed the door and took off toward the house, then turned back. He opened the door and asked, "Where *are* we going? Which hotel?"

Crap! I needed to think of something fast, something from 1960. "Oh, uh, the Peabody. Do you know where it is?"

Elvis laughed. "Of course, I know where the Peabody is, I

went to senior prom there!" He closed the door and headed for the house.

How are you going to make this happen, Maggie? I started the engine and turned the heater on full blast. I fished around in the glove compartment for a tissue or napkin to blow my nose and wipe my face. OK. Dad was staying at the Peabody. It's a busy hotel and maybe there will be enough Elvis fans who will recognize him and keep him occupied with autographs while I steal away and have a pretend meeting with my dad.

I was quiet as we drove downtown. Plotting. Elvis was listening and singing along to music on the radio. He broke our silence: "Are you worried that your dad won't let you come back to Graceland with me?"

"No, I think he'll be OK with it." I paused to fabricate. "I was just thinking of how busy he is and what if he's not able to see us?" I hated deceiving Elvis.

"I'm sure he'll make time for his precious daughter. Otherwise, you can just leave a note with his secretary." He laughed at that.

As we got close to Union Avenue and the Peabody, I attempted to include Elvis' celebrity status into my escalating ruse. Surely he could not just pull up to the front of the hotel like everyone else without causing a scene. "Elvis," I began. "Do we need to go into some back entrance so your fans don't get all excited when they see you? Or maybe you wait in some parking garage while I run in?"

"I don't think that'll be necessary. Besides, I think I'll have the Peabody call Mr. Lansky. He can keep me occupied while you see your Dad."

"Who's Mr. Lansky?"

"You really aren't from around here, are you? Bernard Lansky is owner of Lansky Brothers, where I buy nearly all my clothes."

I felt washed over with relief. Maybe I would not have to introduce Elvis to my dad after all!

We pulled up to the front of the hotel, which was quiet as far as guests coming and going. The valets jumped to attention when they saw who was driving. They practically fell over each other to see who was going to get to drive Elvis Presley's car to its parking spot.

We entered the Peabody with little fanfare, due in part, I imagine, to the fact that there were no young girls waiting around in the lobby. We approached the front desk. Elvis took the lead. "Good afternoon," he said politely to the receptionist. "I have a special favor to ask."

"Of course, Mr. Presley. How may we assist you?" he responded.

"Could you please give Mr. Lansky a call? Tell him Elvis is over at the Peabody with a little time to kill and would like to see a selection of his latest men's fashions."

"Of course," he said and picked up the hotel phone. "Oh, and my friend here needs to see her dad," Elvis added. He picked up a newspaper from the counter and headed to a seating area. Maybe this was going to turn out just fine.

While the front desk receptionist scurried to arrange Elvis' appointment, I headed up the elevators, acting like I knew where I was going. I figured that's where the guest rooms were and Elvis would assume I was going up to see my dad.

I took my time about it; I actually hit all of the elevator buttons once inside so it would stop on every floor. I hate when people do that, but this time I welcomed the opportunity to burn some time.

I eventually got off on the 8th floor and wandered up and down the hallway for a few minutes. Thankfully, I didn't pass anyone who might have wondered what I was up to. I barely remembered that this was 1960 and people weren't as suspicious of each other as they are today.

When I felt like enough time had passed, I headed back down to the lobby, psyching myself up for more deception as I filled Elvis in on my supposed paternal meet-up.

When the elevator returned me to the lobby, Elvis was not there. The newspaper was on the table in front of where he sat, but he was nowhere in sight. I inquired about him at the front desk. "Yes! Maggie, right?" I nodded. "Mr. Presley asked me to escort you to his room."

"Oh," I said, a little surprised. "Did he check in to a room?"

"No, but we offered him a courtesy room for his meeting with Mr. Lansky, who arrived a few minutes ago. I'll take you to them."

Wow. When the King calls, people roll out the red carpet.

Elvis' courtesy room was on the sixth floor. The front desk associate knocked and a young man answered, wary of opening the door all the way. I heard Elvis in the background, "If that's a pretty girl named Moody, let her in."

I laughed and replied loudly: "What if her real name is Maggie?"

"Let her in, too."

I thanked my Peabody escort and entered the room, closing the door behind me. Elvis stepped out of the bathroom in a different outfit than he wore to the Peabody, a unique black and pink combination.

"What do you think?" Elvis asked. This was how Elvis Presley shopped.

"I like it. Very... you."

Another gentleman was busy moving men's clothes around on the two hotel beds. "Maggie, this is Mr. Lansky and his sales associate Steven.

Mr. Lansky reached out to shake my hand. "Call me Bernard," he said. "Otherwise I start looking around for my father."

It was amazing to me how Elvis lived and how just about every moment with him was unpredictable. I had begun our car ride in a near panic over how I was going to introduce Elvis to a man who did not exist at this hotel. Now, it was suddenly about trying on clothes.

After Elvis came out of the bathroom in another ensemble, he asked me, "How's your Pop?"

"Well, I didn't actually get to see him," I replied, letting the deception continue as I was careful to cover my tracks. "He's taking a deposition so he could not be disturbed. But I did go to the room and write a long note to him about how I'm doing, what I'm doing and that I'm going to stay with you for a couple more days until New Year's Eve."

"Well, alright. That's good news. I'm going to try on a few more duds then we'll head back to Graceland."

Whew. Mission accomplished.

CHAPTER 12

Love Me Tender

At the kitchen counter, we had just started eating a dinner of meatloaf and mashed potatoes slathered with mushroom gravy when the phone rang. Alberta answered, "Presley residence, Alberta speaking. How may I help you?" Pause. "Yes, Mr. Colonel. I'll fetch Mr. Elvis for you."

She put the phone on hold and turned to Elvis, who gave her a half-hearted scowl. "Aw, VO5, can't you see I'm eating?" he complained. "Why does the Colonel have to call and interrupt my meal?"

Vernon was sitting with us. "I'll take it, son," he said. "Alberta, I'll talk to the Colonel in the dining room." He got up and headed there.

"Colonel Parker, right?" I said. I couldn't help it; I was mesmerized by this world of people I had only previous read about.

"Yes, my manager," he answered snidely. "But I don't discuss my business affairs with girls and I don't discuss business when I'm eating."

Ouch. "Sorry," I said softly. I stared at my plate. Elvis nudged it slightly to the left. He was playful but surely spoiled and set in his ways.

We ate in silence, except for the regular sounds of a busy, made-to-order kitchen. I savored the taste of mushroom gravy over everything and occupied my thoughts with figuring out what the Colonel was working on now. It was late 1960. I knew the next movie after *Wild in the Country* would be *Blue Hawaii* so it could be the recording sessions for the movie soundtrack. And, Elvis would do something very important for history in 1961: he would perform a benefit concert in Honolulu to help raise the rest of the funding needed to complete the Pearl Harbor memorial for the USS Arizona battleship.

We were finished eating by the time Vernon returned. "Son, the Colonel needs to speak to you, too," he said. "He's still on the line."

"I'll take it in my office," Elvis replied and started heading upstairs. To me, he said, "Why don't you come up with me and find something on TV while I talk to the Colonel."

I followed him up the stairs, surprised that he wouldn't rather keep me separate from business matters. He headed to the office and I went into his bedroom to turn the dial and see what was playing on the networks. *My Three Sons* was wrapping up on ABC. *The Untouchables* crime drama was next.

I was dozing off a little on the bed, listening to *The Untouchables*, when Elvis stormed into the room and startled me. He did not look happy. On second thought, he was steaming mad.

"Goddamnit!" He slammed the door behind him and started pacing the room. I sat up on the bed. "Colonel has another shitty movie script he wants me to read with stupid songs, no plot and no real chance for acting like I've been asking for ever since *King Creole!* Just a chance for him to crank out another blockbuster and spend my money." *Whoa.* I knew that Elvis disliked a lot of the movies he made. And I knew what *he* did not yet: there would be a total of 31 of them.

Elvis continued his rant. "Doesn't that sonofabitch know

how much I hate musicals?" I was unsure what to say, lest I get myself in trouble again, so I just listened. However, my mind was churning with things to say: *Yes, Elvis, some of your movies are lacking in substance but they make people happy! We all just want to spend a couple of hours with you. We don't care what you're doing. We just want to see you smile and sing and swagger.* "Not that I care, but you're thinking something. What are you thinking?" Elvis interrupted my thoughts.

I looked at him cautiously. His mood scared me. I carefully weighed my words before I spoke: "I was just thinking about work and how often times it's something you don't really want to do but you have to because it's a means to an end."

He stopped his pacing, sat on a chair near the bed and leaned toward me. "I make a lot of money and keep a lot of people happy so I shouldn't have to do anything I don't want to," he said emphatically.

"I don't disagree with you, Elvis, but that's not really true about life, is it? Everyone has things we don't want to do or don't want to deal with. But we have to. Those are the crosses God gives us to bear. You have a great many gifts, Elvis. But God will give you crosses to carry, too."

I stopped talking, fearing I'd gone too far with a man who makes it clear he has no use for a woman's point of view. Elvis looked down at the carpet and back up at me, still stewing in his anger. He was steadily tapping one foot on the floor.

I slid off the bed and reached over to touch his hand. "Do you hate going to the movie sets? Memorizing your lines? Acting? Singing? All of your beautiful co-stars? Do you hate all of these things, Elvis?"

"Well, when you put it that way, no, I don't, except for getting up early in the morning." He paused, then sighed. "I just want to do something more important. I want to be taken seriously as an actor. Like James Dean. Why can't the Colonel find me movies like *Rebel Without a Cause?* Or *East of Eden?*"

He had a point. "I think you should ask the Colonel to do just that. I think it's a perfect idea, Elvis. Tell the Colonel what you want to do to earn money. I think you have incredible acting potential!"

He kissed my hand and said, "And until then, I should just pick up my crosses and carry 'em, huh?"

I smiled. "That's certainly a good way to look at it. Say a prayer. Tell God what you wish for. Then tell the Colonel." I winked and squeezed his hand.

"You're different than the other girls, Moody."

"Maybe. Maybe not." He dove out of the chair and on top of me for another romantic tumble.

Make no mistake. Elvis comes alive with the night. We were relaxing on his bed, watching TV. Elvis had changed channels to Tennessee Ernie Ford's variety show on NBC. I could have easily called it a night. But not Elvis. It was as if a switch was flipped and he was full of energy.

"Let me see those sunglasses," Elvis said, sitting up and bouncing around on the bed. "I've never seen anything like 'em." They were sticking out of my new purse on the nightstand. I handed the glasses to him. He put them on and I couldn't help but smile knowing that he's actually the guy who would make them famous. "How do I look?"

"You look great, Elvis. A real trendsetter."

He got up and walked to a mirror, moving his head from side to side to see how they looked. "They're pretty strange, like they belong with a costume."

I giggled. "They do. You got me. I just couldn't give them up after a good Halloween gag."

Elvis pulled the glasses down his nose and looked at me the

way a librarian does. "Moody, you are one strange girl." He took off the glasses and placed them on his nightstand.

"Where are we going tonight?" Elvis asked.

I was thinking: Why go anywhere; let's just stay right here in each other's arms and see what happens.

"Any ideas?" he inquired again.

"I'm game for whatever you want to do, Elvis."

"Game." He paused, thinking. "That's it! Game night. A war on wheels. Tonight, Moody, we're going roller skating!" Elvis picked up the phone on the nightstand and called the guys to get the plans going. He was like a child, all excited and animated. It was fun to watch and I couldn't help but match his enthusiasm. After all, I was about to have another adventure with the King of Rock 'n Roll.

Elvis started to change clothes and suggested I do the same. As I headed downstairs to Patsy's room where my new clothes were, I wondered if I could still roller skate – it had been years since I had.

I changed into another of my new outfits, a green plaid skirt and pink sweater. Skating in a skirt – this ought to be interesting.

It's going to be another late night, I thought, staring at my reflection in the mirror. I have read about how Elvis would rent out the Rainbow Rollerdrome rink in Memphis after hours so he and his friends could have the place to themselves for some skating fun. After hours means after midnight. Whew! Wake up, Maggie.

We piled into several cars for the drive to the Rainbow. Elvis wanted me by his side and I was pleased to oblige. He was talking to Gene in the back seat about how he was going to take out Sonny in a game of War.

"War sounds ominous, Elvis. What is the object of the game?" I asked.

"Well, just as in any war, there are two sides. In our war, the object of the game is to knock down more guys on the opposing team than they knock down on yours. Sort of a last man standing concept."

"Ouch!" I shuddered. "Elvis, I don't want to skate in the War, I might get hurt."

He laughed. Gene and his date in the back seat laughed, too. "Don't worry, Moody, you're not allowed to play War. Because you're right… you might get hurt."

We did some regular roller skating when we first arrived. Elvis paid the DJ to stay late and play music. He and I skated around together, holding hands. I was transported back to my teen years when I did this with my friends. Back then, we would have killed to skate with a boy as handsome as Elvis Presley!

Other guys and girls paired up as well. Red was with his girlfriend Pat Boyd, which I thought was especially sweet because they would get married in July 1961. They must be made for each other, I thought, as they skated around – they're still married.

I was skating fairly well but generally felt wobbly and off balance. Every time I swooned forward or backward or threw my other arm out to balance myself, Elvis cracked up. It was fun to see him smile and hear the sound of his laugh, but the enjoyment was mixed with my efforts not to fall on my ass.

After a few couples' skates, everyone headed off the rink. The snack bar was open so we ordered sodas and popcorn, plus a few hot dogs and pretzels. I noticed the guys skate over to a big equipment bin, where they started reaching in and putting on elbow pads, knee pads, chin guards. Patsy noticed the look of surprise on my face. "It's a good thing they get suited up for War, Maggie," she said with a laugh.

And then War broke out. It was interesting but difficult to watch, especially when you could foresee that someone was about to take a major hit. Some of the guys flew through the air before landing, hard, on the rink. Once a guy was knocked down, he was out of the War.

Not surprisingly, Elvis was always one of the last men standing. Some of his closest friends were comfortable with trying to take him down, but mostly, the object of this game, as with the many other activities, was to keep Elvis happy.

Once Red was out of the current game of War, he came over to where I was watching. Pat had joined the others across the way. My nerves were instantly jangled. I still didn't know if he said something to Elvis about his suspicions. "Maggie, did you check in with your father about spending another evening at Graceland?"

"I'm 29, Red, I already told you that. I don't need my dad's permission to go out at night."

"Where exactly is your father, anyway?" he continued to bait me.

"He's here on business."

"What kind of business?"

I was getting annoyed. "Isn't a bodyguard supposed to stand around and *quietly* watch over his keep?" I sounded braver than I felt.

"I told you once, Maggie. You'd better start answering my

questions or I'll talk to Elvis about you and how the pieces of your story are not matching up." *Maybe he didn't say anything to Elvis yet.*

"My father is a lawyer, Red. He's here working on a case that will go to trial soon. We don't talk about his cases. It's not ethical. I just know he's busy taking depositions and stuff like that. And besides, Elvis took me to see him today and everything is fine." There. That should shut him up.

"Where is he working?"

Trying to keep my cool, I replied, "Some law firm downtown."

"Where downtown?"

"I don't know, Red! I told you, we don't talk about his job." I was exasperated. Telling lies is not my specialty. My head started spinning.

"Where are you staying while in Memphis?"

"We're staying at the Peabody," I said with confidence. "Ask Elvis if you don't believe me."

Red probably would have continued his interrogation of me but suddenly Elvis saved the day, skating up to where we were, running his skates into the wall and grabbing me for a quick kiss. He gave Red a look and I figured it meant that Red should find something else to do because Elvis was not fond of the boys talking to his girls. "Red, you'd better tighten those laces because I'm coming after you in the next round!" Elvis said, rubbed noses with me and skated away as fast as he had arrived.

I exhaled deeply and walked over to a table where Ray, Patsy and some girls were sitting. I joined them for snacks and cheering on the skaters. It felt good to sit down because my legs were shaky. "What do you think, Maggie?" Patsy asked.

"Of Elvis?" She nodded. "He's amazing, all of this is amazing," I said as I watched him skate at full speed. I lowered my voice so only she could here me. "Thank you very much for being so kind. I'll never forget it."

Patsy patted my hand. "I'm not sure why I took you under my wing, Maggie. There's something special about you, like a breath of fresh air. My cousin seems to sense that, too."

I put my other hand on top of hers. "I'm grateful. Really, I am."

The soldiers of War eventually wore themselves out and joined the rest of us at the snack bar tables. All in all, the first aid tech Elvis had on call did not have too many casualties, but there were some scrapes and cuts to tend to.

Some of the guys ordered snacks, but Elvis declared, "The food is better at Graceland. Let's get a move on." We all headed for the benches to shed our skates and leave the Rainbow.

Elvis and I had the car to ourselves on the way home, which was a nice surprise. We played a silly game, kissing at every red light. I started the game, recalling it from my high school days. Elvis caught on quickly and would slow on approach to an intersection with a green light, hoping it would turn from yellow to red. I'm sure the guys behind us were wondering why the guy with a passion for racing and competition was taking his sweet time.

When we arrived back at the mansion and parked the car, Elvis said, "Red light." He leaned in for a kiss.

Playfully, I said, "I don't think so. Aren't you stretching the rules of the game?"

"Maybe." We kissed. I breathed in the post-War smell of him.

"Speaking of traffic lights, how will the rest of evening go?"

Elvis thought for a minute. "Well… we're at a red light now." We kissed again. "Let's go inside and see what everyone else is doing. Then follow the same plan as we did last night to meet upstairs. That's sort of a yellow light, using caution." He laughed at his pun. "Does that sound like a plan?"

"I'll give your plan a green light, Elvis. Green as in go." I exited the car, barely able to contain my excitement. *Now who's awake with the night!*

We joined the others in the basement but looking around, saw that everyone was pooped. Elvis didn't waste much time. "I think we could all use some rest after the roller skating. I'm going up. Good night."

He patted me on the hand as he got up from his seat. I tried to act inconspicuous but who, really, was going to believe I was not headed up after him? I didn't dare make eye contact with Red.

The same sense of relief I saw last night washed over the group again and people started heading up and out, to their rooms or their cars. I lost myself in the shuffle and went into one of the basement bathrooms to kill a few minutes. *Will it happen tonight? Or will Elvis fall asleep again?* The anticipation made me nervous. *Another night with the King!* What woman wouldn't kill to be in my place.

I opened the bathroom door and made my way upstairs. The first floor was vacant. I took a deep breath, smiled and went upstairs to Elvis' room and whatever was about to happen.

When I entered his bedroom, Elvis was in pajamas, reading the paper in bed. Or rather, he was writing on it. "Can I get you a pad of paper from somewhere?" I asked.

"No, this will do. When I think of things, I write 'em down before I forget." Elvis put down his pen and tore the top inch or two of the newspaper off in a long strip. He then started rolling it up.

"Are you going to smoke that?" I said, laughing and heading into the bathroom to get changed into something more comfortable.

"No, but I'm gonna smoke you when you get back out here. Hurry up!"

When I came out of the bathroom, Elvis sitting on the bed and reaching for his bottle of red pills on the nightstand. *Oh no, don't take any!* "Elvis, what do you say we don't go to sleep for a little while?" As I said that, I walked into the space between his legs and held his face in my hands. I kissed him on the forehead.

He said, "I wasn't going to take any Reds yet. Unless you wanted to." He kissed me on the lips.

"I don't need them," I said, in between kisses. "Because I can get high on you." He leaned back on to the bed, pulling me on top of him. *Was this really going to happen?*

We continued kissing for a few minutes. I've always enjoyed kissing boys but Lord, did I love kissing Elvis Presley! He was gentle, yet a bit controlling. He was in charge, leading me first with long, sweet kisses. Not just on the lips but cheeks, eyelids, and ears.

As our desire heated, Elvis used his tongue. More passionate, open-mouthed kissing made us start to squirm around on the bed. I could feel his erection once again and delighted in the fact that there were no pills to send him to sleep.

I undid a few buttons on his pajama top. Elvis reached up and pulled back the covers as he scooted toward the pillows. "C'mere, sexy." He invited me into his bed and as I climbed in, he pulled loose the belt on my robe. I had a little surprise for him – nothing. "I didn't know it was your birthday... but now I do because you're wearing your birthday suit."

Elvis wiggled out of his top and I tossed the robe on the floor. "Why, yes, it is my birthday," I said, reaching under the blankets to put my hand around his manhood. The look of pleasure on his face was exhilarating. "And now it's time for me to blow out the candle." Elvis let out a groan. I went deeper into the bedding.

"Moody," Elvis moaned a minute or two later. "Not yet." I crawled out from under the covers, feeling like a vixen. I joined him up on the pillows and our eyes met. "You're so goddamn sexy," he said.

"Why thank you," I whispered. We were both on our sides facing each other. I smiled and touched his face. "Oh, and now I can kiss those dimples again!" As he kissed them both, I giggled.

Elvis coaxed me on to my back and lowered a hand beneath the covers. I closed my eyes and relished every second of his touch. He caressed me everywhere. His beautiful face had taken on such passion. Elvis was in the heat of the moment. His lips covered mine. We kissed again and again. "Elvis," I whispered. "I want you."

"I want you, too."

Elvis Presley climbed on top of me. My heart was attempting to beat its way out of my chest. I wrapped my arms around him. Slowly, sexily, we made love. It was... *enchanting*.

When it was over, Elvis relaxed a bit, still on top of me. He kissed me several times on the neck and lips. Our eyes met. "Happy birthday," he said, and rolled over to lay beside me, both of us now on our backs. He reached for my hand and we lay like that, both staring at the ceiling, while the pace of our heartbeats slowed.

I turned my head toward him and said, "I'm glad we did this."

"What a coincidence. I am, too."

I was blissful. "This has been one of the most amazing days of my life," I said. "Next to yesterday."

Elvis turned to look at me. "Yesterday?" he asked. "What was better about yesterday?"

"That was the day I met you."

Facing each other now, we kissed again and joined hands. The King of Rock 'n Roll closed his eyes to slumber. It was peaceful and that is how we remained. As I dozed off, still smiling, I wondered if this was a rare occasion, Elvis falling asleep without the aid of a pill.

CHAPTER 13

Can't Help Falling in Love

When my eyes fluttered open, my first thought of the new day was this: *I had sex with Elvis Presley.* I remember and it was real. It could not have been a dream. I looked around, still groggy but with a nagging curiosity to see where I would start this day. Especially since the past couple of days had begun with unbelievable surprises.

I was relieved to learn that I had again awakened in Elvis' bedroom. The slumbering King of Rock 'n Roll was beside me under the blankets. I know I should probably be anxious to return to the reality I know best. But I wasn't quite finished with this place. Or him. And perhaps fate agreed with me.

I looked at the clock. It was after 2 p.m. I began my third day at Graceland much like yesterday. I left the handsome king to his dreams and freshened up in his bathroom. I went down to the kitchen in my robe for more of Alberta's mouth-watering morning fare. It was well after lunchtime, but she knew to have breakfast items for the late risers of the house. Once again, I devoured bacon, eggs over easy, and this time, fried green tomatoes. Animal fats, carbs and cholesterol. But when in Rome – or when in Memphis – do what the Memphians do.

When I went back upstairs to see if Elvis was awake, he was still sleeping so I decided to take a shower and wash my hair. The hot water felt great. As I stood beneath the flow, the water hypnotized me such that I had no idea Elvis was in the bathroom with me until I was hit with a blast of cold. I shrieked, jumping out of the way of the showerhead, only to realize it had come from him, standing there laughing at me, with the suspect empty drinking glass in his hand. "That was cold!" I said, attempting a little modesty by covering my chest with my arms.

"I can tell," he replied and offered what was in his other hand, a robe. I turned off the faucet and took the robe, grateful for its cover.

"I hope I didn't wake you."

"You didn't. Mother Nature did." As he headed back to the bedroom, he said, "Take your time doing all that girly stuff. I won't kick you out yet."

"Thank you," I replied and proceeded to get ready for another day with the King.

Later, I grabbed the bathroom doorknob to rejoin Elvis in the bedroom but paused when I heard him talking. Maybe someone came up to see him. Not sure if I should stay in here? That made the most sense to me so I halted.

"I miss you, Nungen," Elvis said. "I close my eyes and see your beautiful face every day. I can't wait to see you again." Pause. "I'm working on it, Cilla. Daddy and I are working on a plan for you to visit and we'll speak to him about it real soon. I promise." *He's talking to Priscilla, his future wife!* Pause. "I want you to smile, Little One. I don't hear a smile in your voice. No sadness. Only happiness." Pause. "Tell me you love me, Satnin." *He has a lot of pet names for her!* "I love you, too. I have to go now. I'll call you again soon. Behave yourself and do good in school. Goodbye, Nungen."

I couldn't contain my excitement at this moment I'd stumbled into. I opened the bathroom door at pretty much the exact moment Elvis hung up the phone. I was unsure if I should act like I knew he was on the phone. Curiosity got the best of me.

"Elvis, you have yourself a stable of women, don't you?" I said, then regretted it because he gave me a look. "I'm sorry, it's none of my business. In fact, I feel like I'm in the way. I know there are other girls who want to see you… others who are much more important to you. Elvis, I can go, if you want me to. No hard feelings. It's been wonderful getting to know you but I wouldn't feel right if I got in the way of something… or someone."

Elvis reached for my hand and pulled me onto the bed with him. "Well, listen to the Moody girl blabbing on and on. What do you say we try a little less talking?"

Ha! He's lobbing me a softball and doesn't even know it. I responded: "And a little more action?" That made him smile and we soon melted into one another. *Way to change the subject, King. You really do live in a league of your own.*

After Elvis had showered, dressed and come downstairs to eat, he said he had an announcement to make. He looked marvelous in his new black and pink ensemble from Lansky's. I was glad I chose to wear one of my new dresses, this one a light purple print. I looked around at his friends and no one seemed too worried about what he was about to say. Vernon nodded at his son. "Today, we're going to give back to our community," Elvis said. "The Lord God has been good to us and this is the season of giving."

Since Elvis' return from the Army, he and Vernon had been working to set up a special donation day at Graceland. Of course I knew what Elvis and Vernon may not have known at this point: it was to become a longstanding annual event. The Presleys would eventually select 50 Memphis charities and worthy causes each year. Representatives from each of these organizations would be invited to Graceland on a day between

Christmas Day and New Year's Day. Elvis would sign and distribute checks to each of the groups in an amazing show of generosity. And not once did Elvis or his father try to garner publicity for their donations. They simply wanted to share the good that had been given to them with others.

The world will never know just how much money Elvis gave away. He paid hospital bills for some, he paid off debts for others and much more.

The donation event took place in Vernon's office. I stood in the background with Patsy. All of the charities, including the Crippled Children's Hospital, March of Dimes and Memphis Boys Town, were very happy and grateful. Many of them were star struck but you could tell they were trying not to be. "I feel so privileged to witness this," I whispered to Patsy.

"It's very touching," she agreed.

I could tell Elvis got a big kick out of helping others. My admiration grew as I watched him hand out checks, shake hands and smile for photos. Somehow, the local paper had found out and Elvis seemed fine with the reporter and his camera.

As the charity event wound down, I headed to the basement, assuming that's where the group would gather until we figured out what was next on Elvis' agenda. The basement was empty except for my favorite bodyguard Red. "Hi, Red." was all I said, trying to sound friendly. He kept his gaze on me but said nothing for a moment.

"I took a drive downtown this morning, Maggie. To the Peabody Hotel." I froze. "The front desk told me there weren't any Coyles staying there. Not a Mister Coyle. Not his daughter, Maggie. Does your father have a different last name?"

"Red, listen. I know you're suspicious of me. But can't you see that I'm not a bad person? I don't mean any harm, especially to Elvis. I know it's your job to protect him. It's just that… I know you probably won't believe me but you can ask Patsy. I've been having some trouble remembering what lead me to Graceland. I don't know if someone slipped me a pill or what, but I honestly don't remember how I got here and Patsy just took me under her wing and then I met Elvis and he's been so nice and I'm just taking things a few hours at a time, hoping everything will sort itself out." I paused to catch my breath. *I must sound crazy!*

Red was listening but his expression had not softened so I doubted my rambling was doing any good. "Red, please, you have to believe me. I'm just a girl who is confused while at the same time trying to live in the moment because she's spending time with Elvis Presley!"

Red stared at me for a few more seconds then said, "That's a steaming pile of crap, Maggie," he said emphatically. "You lied to Elvis. Today is your last day at Graceland." With that, he got up and left the basement.

Elvis and the boys traipsed down eventually and turned the TV on to watch *The Adventures of Rin Tin Tin*. I couldn't concentrate after Red's threat. He was starting to scare me. I remember Red saying in an interview that he got so mad at a guy once he broke the guy's foot and threatened to work his way up. He was reacting to someone who provided Elvis with the pills he was dependent on and it was right before Red got fired for trying to get Elvis to go to rehab. On one hand, I feel for the guy. On the other, I don't want to be on his bad side.

Feeling nervous, I decided to go upstairs and wander around the first floor a little, at least as much as I would be allowed to. I thought about having something to eat in the kitchen but didn't have much of an appetite.

I can't believe how emotional this experience is. No wonder Elvis nicknamed me Moody. All my life when my emotions were high, I talked to my mom. I've been thinking about her during this experience. If I've been sent back to 1960, she's still alive, right? Could I find her somehow and see her again?

This stuff is really messing with my head! I'm having the time of my life, experiencing life with Elvis Presley, but because the circumstances of how I got here are strange and scary, I can't help but miss home and what I know.

I walked into the music room and sat down at the white baby grand piano. I knew that Elvis spent private moments in here, playing and singing gospel tunes. Mom's favorite song was "Over the Rainbow" from *The Wizard of Oz*. I had enough piano lessons when I was a kid to remember how to plunk it out, so I did, singing quietly to myself:

Somewhere over the rainbow, way up high
there's a land that I've heard of once in a lullaby

I started humming and playing the rest when I heard someone in the room behind me. I turned around and it was Elvis, leaning on the doorjamb. Ah, just the sight of him made me weak!

"Has my Moody Girl disappeared somewhere over the rainbow?"

"It was Mom's favorite song and I'm missing her."

Elvis moved to sit down next to me on the piano bench and I moved over so he could. "I have an idea. Let's sing your mama's favorite song," he said as he placed his hands on the keys.

He began playing the song so beautifully and singing:

Somewhere over the rainbow, way up high
there's a land that I've heard of once in a lullaby

Elvis nudged me with his elbow while he continued playing. He wants me to sing? My face flushed. But from somewhere within me, I summoned the courage:

Somewhere over the rainbow, skies are blue
and the dreams that you dare to dream really do come true

Now Elvis sang:

Someday I'll wish upon a star
and wake up where the clouds are far behind me

Elvis looked my way and I continued:

Where troubles melt like lemon drops away above the chimney tops
that's where you'll find me

Aahh, my voice broke! Thinking of my mother, my throat had tightened. Trying to sing while trying not to cry hurts.

I shook my head but Elvis continued with his sweet voice and effortless piano:

Somewhere over the rainbow, blue birds fly
If birds fly over the rainbow, why then oh why can't I?

He played a short bridge of instrumental music while I got it back in gear. What a miracle moment I am in. We sang the last line together:

If happy little blue birds fly beyond the rainbow
why oh why can't I?

When the song was over, Elvis put his arm around me again and we sat quietly for a few minutes. I concentrated on breathing deeply to still the hurt in my heart. I didn't want to lose it completely.

I'm not 100 percent sure but as we sat in the silence of the music room, I think Elvis may have gotten a little teary-eyed, too. He recovered quickly, though, and said, "I wonder if my mama is somewhere up in heaven sitting next to your mama, listening to us sing."

I answered, "I think they are Elvis. They're watching us, smiling and giving us the strength to go on in spite of their absence in our lives."

A few more seconds of silence. "Well, I don't know about you but performing makes me hungry. Let's go to the kitchen and put VO5 to work."

Our song to our mothers was over. *Mom, did you see? Did you hear?*

CHAPTER 14

Trouble

After everyone had a late dinner of burnt bacon sandwiches, with mustard on toasted rye, and a delicious banana pudding, we gathered back down in the basement. The TVs were on but the music was turned up, a Jackie Wilson song followed by Sam Cooke.

Elvis challenged Jerry to a game of billiards. Sonny, over at the wet bar, pulled out two bottles of champagne followed by several champagne glasses, which he proceeded to line up in a row on the bar. I knew Elvis was not a big drinker and didn't allow his staffers to drink in his presence so I was curious to see how this would play out. George, eyeing Elvis at the pool table, said, "Sonny, it's December 30th not 31st. You're a day early."

Elvis looked up from his game and replied, "Ain't nothing wrong with starting the celebration a little early. Go ahead and pop those corks, Sonny. And bring me a lit cigar while you're at it." He looked at me and winked. I have such a crush on this man! He looked sexy once again, in an ivory sweater and brown pants. I was wearing brown pants, too. I had changed into my favorite outfit from the spree, the brown and white polka dot set. It felt awesome to be wearing pants and I didn't look too out of place since it was a casual evening.

As they played pool and prepped champagne, I evaluated my situation again. My knowledge of Elvis history told me that he was falling in love with Priscilla, still over in West Germany, and had a Memphis-based girlfriend named Anita Wood. I'm not a jealous person but I don't like to share. Yet here I am… sharing. In fact, I'm third fiddle. Elvis probably has a date with Anita tomorrow night. But he seems to like me and he wants to spend time with me so I guess what I really need to do is live in the moment because Red has been threatening me and who knows how this crooked chapter in my life will end.

My thoughts continued to swirl when Sonny handed me a glass of pre-New Year's Eve champagne. Charlie was helping out and stood by the billiard table with a couple of glasses for Elvis and Jerry. "Just a half glass for you, Jerry, since you're still underage," Charlie said.

After his shot that sank a couple of balls, Elvis took his glass and made his way over by me, a stinky cigar hanging out of his mouth.

George stood up and said, "I propose a toast. In gratitude for Elvis' service to the Army and safe return to Memphis earlier this year. For a successful 1961 of movies and music. And for the privilege all of us have to share these experiences with our best friend. Here's to another prosperous year for Elvis!"

Everyone answered with "Here, here!" and "Cheers!" Elvis moved toward me to intertwine our arms for our first sips of champagne. That gesture included a tobacco-infused kiss and he was gone, back to his game of pool. He set his glass down to take his shot and I noticed later that he never returned to it. Elvis Presley was not a drinker.

The champagne made the rest of us a little sillier and while Patsy and I were giggling about something, I overheard Billy say to Sonny, "The champagne came early, why not the fireworks?" Elvis had wrapped up his pool game, victorious once again.

"Oh, wow, fireworks!" I said to Patsy as the group made their way to the screened-in porch and outside on the back driveway. Billy and Red had hauled out a bunch of fireworks and the bangs and pops soon ensued.

"Make that *competitive* fireworks, Maggie," Patsy added. It took me a moment to realize that the guys, like most everything they do, had indeed turned fireworks into a competition. It seemed a bit dangerous but they thrilled to that.

"Ladies, let's go onto the porch and watch from a safer distance," Patsy said. That sounded like a good idea so we followed her.

Some of the Graceland staff came out to watch the battle, too, including Vernon. It was pretty funny; they launched bottle rockets at each other from makeshift tubes. Again, neither smart nor safe. But entertaining. Chris would get a kick out of this, I thought.

Chris. Where was he now? Would I ever see him again? Could he possibly wake up in the basement closet like I did? I'd been in the basement several times over the past few days but hadn't returned to the little storage room where I first emerged to this place and time. Could that closet be a portal? I can't believe I'm having these thoughts.

BANG! That one startled me back to reality. It sounded like an M80. The guys were cracking up. So far, no injuries. The smell of gunpowder was prominent. I looked around and saw that there were plenty of spectators. I excused myself to use the restroom but instead headed to the basement closet.

My heart was pounding in my chest as I descended the basement stairs. I had no idea what I was going to find. When I reached to door to the closet, it hit me like a ton of bricks. *This will be Jerry's room!* Hard to believe I had just looked at this door a couple of days ago on the Graceland tour.

I turned the knob and stepped slowly into the closet. It was the same as I remembered it. Boxes, outdoor furniture, a Christmas tree. Where was it that I woke up? There. In the back. Between the coiled hose and the milk crates. But how did I go from my hotel room bed in 2006 to this place? I crept a little closer. Baby steps. I was unsure if I would suddenly fall into a rabbit hole or something.

Suddenly, there was shouting and screaming above me. Footsteps. Running into the house. Oh no! Someone got hurt by the fireworks! Jarred by the commotion back to this reality, I quickly made my way out of the closet and closed the door behind me. No one was running down the basement steps but as I started to climb them, Elvis appeared in the doorway at the top. "Moody! There you are! I've been calling for you! Get up here, we started the house on fire!"

"What? Oh no!" I sprinted up the stairs.

"It's OK. We've got it under control. Don't think we'll need to call the fire department. There's just a lot of smoke and we want everyone outside while we plug in some fans and air the place out."

When I got to the stop of the stairs and Elvis grabbed me by the hand, I saw that he was right. Smoke was filtering through the kitchen and the back porch. The smell of gunpowder was prevalent as we moved toward the back door. "What happened?" I asked.

"I love him like a brother but Gene's got bad aim. He fired a bundle of bottle rockets and hit the wood pile." Elvis took me around to the scene of the crime. "We didn't notice until the wood caught fire and we saw the flames."

"Thank the Lord no one was hurt!" I said. I turned from the woodpile to him and gave him a stern look. "I know you guys like to have battles and competitions, but you know the saying, 'When you play with fire…'"

Elvis finished the phrase: "You get burned. But the only thing burning tonight is some 'ole hunks of wood. And *you*, when I get you back upstairs!" Elvis, ever the flirt, pulled me close to him.

"Oh really! Well, we'll see who gets who all *fired* up, won't we?" I yanked his shirt collar closer to me so I could plant a big kiss on his lips.

We were walking together in the backyard and Elvis had his arm around my shoulder. Ever true to himself, despite the hour Elvis was ready for more activity. He stopped and turned to the rest of the group. "Let's go cruisin' for Christmas lights. I like lookin' at Christmas lights. Moody here likes 'em, too. Anybody else like Christmas lights?" There were several nods and verbal agreements. Elvis declared, "Alan, you take the lead. Show us some of the best light displays in Memphis." Alan looked at Lamar. "Go ahead, Alan. Light the way!" Lamar said with a laugh, probably glad it wasn't on him to figure where to lead us.

The group sprang into action. As we made our way to the cars in the driveway and carport, I caught myself starting to yawn and stifled it. I was tired but couldn't help but wonder if I would I get to spend another night with Elvis. Sleep can wait if I'm going to get more quality time with the King!

We piled into the cars and formed a caravan on the way out of the parking lot. Red and Pat were in the backseat of Elvis' car. Red's presence put me on edge. Elvis patted the middle seat next to him when I climbed into the passenger seat so I scooted over to sit next to him and tried to focus on the positive. I hope Red behaves himself.

We drove around Memphis, from Graceland on Highway 51 into the midtown area and Evergreen. I was taken back to my childhood when Dad would pile all of us in the car during the holidays to cruise through the neighborhoods that had the best holiday decorations. Something about things that light up – they're just beautiful. Tonight, they were beautiful as well, but different in 1960. They hadn't invented icicle or netted lights yet. Most homes had single strands of the standard outdoor lights framing the edges of their walls and roofs, and I have to admit these are still my favorites.

"I see your dimples," Elvis said.

"I guess that means I'm smiling. It's all so beautiful. I just love things that light up."

"Well, those dimples really light up your face," he added.

"Thank you." I lay my head on his shoulder and thought, for the hundredth time, this cannot really be happening.

Elvis pulled up to the lead car at a traffic light and gunned his engine. We rolled our windows down and for a moment, I thought we were going to drag race. "Naaah, it's late, I'm just joking," Elvis yelled to Gene. "Plus I know we're all carrying precious cargo so let's just head on home."

"Yeah," Gene yelled. "Save it for the next motorcycle race."

As we all returned to the mansion in separate cars, we gathered in the kitchen to see what the cooks had left for us. I felt closer to Elvis than ever. He was very attentive and charming, and I was like a little fish near the surface of the water, popping up for every morsel he tossed to me.

On the opposite end of the spectrum was Red. While the car ride was uneventful, I could feel the tension between us again when he walked into the kitchen. He would try to catch my eye when Elvis wasn't looking and glare at me or mouth words to me like "I'm on to you." I was becoming anxious. Elvis leaned in and kissed my ear and said, "Tonight, the usual. I'll go upstairs first. Then you join me a little while after that."

Before long, Elvis said good night and went up the back stairs. Red moved a little closer to me. Thinking he intended to take the seat that Elvis just vacated, I moved around in the kitchen so we would not be seated together.

I pretended to eat a snack but was too nervous to be hungry. I started wondering if I was going to be able to make a dash for the stairs without passing Red but at the moment, he was blocking the way. I came up with an exit strategy that would involve me leaving the kitchen to use the first floor bathroom. Then from there, sneaking up the front stairs to Elvis' room.

Everyone was tired and getting up one by one, and saying their good nights before heading off to bed. When George got up to leave, I took advantage of that and headed out of the kitchen and hurried to the guest bathroom. I quickly closed the door and locked it. Whew! I looked at myself in the mirror. Girl, you sure don't look like someone who's about to spend another night with the King of Rock 'n Roll.

I spent a few minutes touching up my face and hair. I listened at the door for any foot traffic and hearing none, quietly opened the door and looked out. I started to tiptoe my way to the front stairs. What happened next was so fast it knocked the wind out of me.

Red had been hiding in the shadows nearby and when he stepped out to block my way, I turned in a haphazard response to get away from him and slammed right into the bannisters, the railing clocking me in the throat. I coughed, trying to refill my lungs. Red was right behind me.

"Red!" I said, turning in the tight space to face him. "You

scared me!"

"Maggie, or whatever your name is, I said this was your last day at Graceland and I meant it." He leaned in until we were nearly nose-to-nose. He was so close I could feel his breath. "You've been lying to Elvis and all of us about your identity. I don't know what you're trying to accomplish other than being a little *whore*, but I will *not* let you hurt Elvis in any way! I've been protecting him from all sorts of people who mean him harm and you will *not* be one of them."

The force of his words made me cry. Tears ran down my cheeks. "Red, please, it's not what you think. I would never, ever hurt Elvis! Honest, I wouldn't!" Red backed up a bit. I edged my way to foot of the stairs. My knees were shaking. I tripped on the first step as I started up.

I turned back to Red and whispered, "I'll explain everything tomorrow, but I have to go now, Red. He's expecting me."

Red replied, in a hushed but threatening tone, "You've got until tomorrow, missy, or I'll sit Elvis down and tell him you're a fraud." He paused and pointed his fingers at me like he was shooting a gun. "Tomorrow… you're finished."

I hurried up the stairs and missed the last one, stumbling again. I caught myself, straightened up, rubbing my neck where I hit the railing. I hope it's not obvious!

I slowly entered Elvis' bedroom, unsure of where he would be. I did not see him in the bedroom so he must be in the bathroom. I rushed to the bed to sit and compose myself. My legs felt like jelly. I did my best to recover but the tears overflowed. I was sure my eye makeup was now a mess so I tried to wipe away the combination of tears and mascara. What am I going to do when he finds out where I came from? He won't believe me! No one will. I can't believe I'm thinking this but… I want to go home. Will I ever get to go home or am I stuck here? I'm scared! *Breathe, Maggie, breathe.*

I heard the bathroom door open and Elvis emerged in his pajamas and robe. He swaggered seductively, jiggling a bottle of baby oil in his hands. But one look at me and he dropped the bottle and rushed to my side. He put his arm around me and took my chin in his hands, turning my face to his. "Maggie! What's the matter? What happened?" He lifted my chin higher and saw my neck. "Your neck! What happened? Did someone touch you? I'll beat him to bloody!" He jumped up but I pulled him back down.

"Elvis, I'm OK. It's OK. Please… don't do anything. It was a… it was an accident."

He held my chin up and turned it from left to right. "For Christ's sake, what kind of accident makes your neck all red and blotchy like this, Maggie? And it looks like you've been crying!" His temper was flaring.

"Let me see," I said. Elvis helped me up to the nearest mirror where I flinched when I saw my neck, my tear-stained face, with eye makeup running down my cheeks. I felt dizzy. The room started spinning and I lost my balance. "Elvis, I need to lie down. I just need to catch my breath. Then everything will be alright."

Elvis led me to the bed and I leaned back into the pillows. He covered me with a blanket and headed for the door. "Elvis, please! Don't leave me! Don't go!" He was gone.

I sat in the quiet, listening for something, anything, hopefully not the sound of Elvis losing this temper on Red or worse, someone else. After what seemed like too long for him to be gone, he returned and started pacing. "I don't know what happened but there's no one down there now and whoever it was had better be long gone!" He took a step closer to the bed, where I was staring at him, wide-eyed. "Start talking, Maggie," he continued. "What happened down there? When I find out, all hell is gonna break loose if someone laid his hands on you!"

I reached for him. "Elvis, please... calm down. Please stay here with me. I don't know how long..." My voice trailed off. I was going to say I don't know how long we have together but changed my mind and added, "I need a cool wash cloth... could you get me one, please?"

Elvis, hands on his hips, glared at me for a second or two. He probably wasn't used to being asked to fetch something. He turned and went into the bathroom, coming out a few moments later with a soft cloth that he had run under the faucet. I sat up and started dabbing at my smeared makeup and sore neck.

"You don't know how long what, Maggie?" He paused, still fuming. "What did you mean when you said that?"

Seconds passed as he waited for my response. I took a deep breath and let it out. "Elvis, I have something to tell you. I'm going to try to explain how I showed up here at Graceland but it might not make sense because I'm still trying to figure it out myself. Please come here and sit next to me and I'll tell you..."

Elvis looked stunned. Before joining me in bed, he went and turned the lock on the bedroom door. I had not seen him do that before. I thought he was confident that no one would ever come into his bedroom without first being invited, but considering what may have been running through his mind, I guess he wanted the extra assurance.

Elvis joined me on the bed. Hoping I got enough makeup off of my face, I put the towel on my neck to cool the skin. We faced each other; he sat cross-legged and upright, stiff. I took his hand in my free one and kissed it, then let go as I started to tell him my story:

"I'm from St. Louis but I'm not here with my dad. I came to Memphis with a friend who's a reporter working on a story." Elvis flinched, as if offended. "He's harmless," I continued. "My friend and I went to Beale Street the other night and we had some drinks and went back to my hotel room." Elvis raised an eyebrow. "My friend had his own room; he didn't stay with me. I fell asleep on the bed in my room but when I woke up… I was here."

"Here?" Elvis asked. "Where here? At Graceland? That makes no sense!"

"I know. But it's the truth. I woke up in the storage room in your basement."

Elvis dropped his head forward and shook it from side to side. "Whoever gave you the drugs you're taking is going to get a beating from me. You, Moody Girl, are off your rocker!" He fell back on the bed and started laughing. I was shocked. This was not the reaction I expected from him.

"Elvis, I'm serious! I don't know how I got to Graceland!"

"You may not know how you got here but you're sure on one helluva trip!" he said, cracking himself up again.

Now I was shaking my head, but felt my mood lighten a bit. "Alright, I was trying to be serious about the situation I'm in but if you're just going to laugh at me…"

Elvis rolled on his side to face me and propped himself up on his elbow. "If you want to be serious, I'll get serious. You lied to me, Moody, for no reason. Beautiful women are always welcome here, whether you came in with one of my friends or a friend of a friend. I don't care. Do you know how many girls try to get inside this place? You didn't need to make up some goofy story about my storage room." He laughed again.

"I'm sorry. I shouldn't have lied. Will you forgive me?" I

reclined to a similar position as his so we were eye to eye. "I was scared and confused when I woke up here but everyone, including, you has been very nice. It's been like a dream." I paused and nodded my head, realizing that this whole thing may be a dream. "You've seen the *Wizard of Oz*, right?" Elvis nodded. "Dorothy went to Oz in a tornado and had a great adventure but at the end of the movie you find out maybe the yellow brick road was a dream?" Elvis nodded again. "I think my great adventure with you at Graceland is just a dream. One I never want to wake up from."

Elvis reached out and pinched my leg, hard.

"Ouch!" I yelled.

"You seem pretty awake to me. Come here." Elvis pulled me to him and kissed me on my forehead and dimples while he whispered, "I ain't no scarecrow, I ain't no tin man and I ain't no lion." He took my hand in his. "But if you follow my yellow brick road," he said and moved our clasped hands down his body, "I'll show you the Wizard." He had me. The little fish just took the bait.

"Show me," I replied, eagerly.

If you asked me which was better, the first time I had sex with Elvis Presley or the second, I would have to claim indecisiveness. The first time will always have distinction. There can't be another first time. Nothing compares to life's wonderful firsts, with their quirky combinations of perfect and imperfect. But the second time was wonderful, too. Elvis was so sexy. Romantic yet silly. His goofy baby talk was parts strange and adorable. He was in command, yet loving. We moved in sync with a familiarity that had grown by a leap in just 24 hours, and our emotions ran high, trailing the events of the day. As long as I live, I'll never forget making love with the King of Rock 'n Roll.

We were lying entwined on his bed, both of us in that tranquil post-sex haze, when Elvis said, "Don't take this the wrong way, Moody." He sat up and reached for the bottle of pills on his nightstand. Then he met my eyes. "I had a great time with you today, and just a few minutes ago." He smiled that famous Elvis grin as he opened the bottle and poured two red pills into his hand. "I don't want you to go anywhere. But I need to get some sleep. Tomorrow is New Year's Eve. 1961 is coming!" Elvis popped the pills into his mouth and followed them with a few gulps of water from a glass. He held the pill bottle out to me. "Want one? We can try to find each other in our dreams."

I was unsure what to do. "No thanks," I replied. "But I'll still look for you in dream land."

We crawled back under the covers together, still naked, and fell asleep. Elvis, because the pills told him to. Me, because I was worn out from my adventure.

When I awoke, I wasn't sure how much time had passed. It seemed the sun was starting to rise and peek through the curtains. My sunglasses were on the nightstand; Elvis must have put them there. I wiggled out of his embrace and put them on to block out the growing daylight. I lay on my back, staring at the ceiling. My thoughts went back to whether I have been dreaming all of this like Dorothy. I'm still here in 1960 but how much time has passed in the present?

I looked over at Elvis, sleeping peacefully. As I tucked his wild flock of hair back from his forehead, I whispered to the sleeping King: "I guess there's no point in telling you that I'm from the future… a future without you."

I lay back on the pillow but my mind would not rest. If this is a dream, why didn't I wake up back in 2006 after I fell asleep? Do dreams go on for days? My thoughts drifted to the basement storage room. I know I didn't imagine that because I was down there last night before the fireworks accident. I tried to quiet my thoughts. I said a prayer. My mind kept returning to the basement. I glanced at the door to Elvis' bedroom. It was locked but I could easily unlock it. Would Red be waiting for me again? My heart beat a little faster. I needed to know about the storage room.

I got up, stepped over the brown and white polka dots on the floor and put on a robe and slippers. I took off the sunglasses and put them in the pocket of my robe. Quietly, I tiptoed to the bedroom door. I kept my eyes on Elvis as I unlocked the door lock. It made a sound but he did not stir. Even if he did, I'm sure he would just tell me to go down for breakfast and he'd see me later after he woke up. The one person I didn't want to wake up or run into now was Red.

As I came downstairs, I could smell the usual smells and hear the usual sounds coming from the kitchen. My stomach growled; my eating schedule was sure off kilter in 1960. Putting aside my urge to go in and eat one of Alberta's hot breakfasts, I quietly made my way down to the basement. I didn't pass anyone on my way, thankfully. Soon I was standing in front of the storage room staring at the door to what would one day be Jerry's little room.

Slowly, I opened the door and headed inside. I looked around at all of the items in the small space. How did I get from 2006 to 1960? I edged my way through the clutter to the back of the closet. What was I looking for, a tiny door like in *Alice in Wonderland?* I must be out of my mind!

And then something very strange happened. The floor seemed to go wobbly on me, like it was neither hard nor flat.

I've never been surfing but imagine that was what it felt like as I tried to keep my balance. Next, I felt a weird vibration in between my ears. I scarcely had time to analyze what was happening before I landed on something soft. Face down. I jerked my head up to breathe. I was staring at a pillow. On a bed. It was not Elvis' bed. And the King was not lying beside me.

CHAPTER 15

Return to Sender

The first sounds I heard were a click, a whirr and a motor running. I looked to my right and saw a wall. I rolled over and saw daylight peeking through the curtains. My duffle bag was on the floor. My duffle bag?

I bolted upright. My mind was foggy. I looked around the room and saw a portrait of Elvis on the wall. Sexy Elvis, in his black leather suit, from the *1968 Comeback Special*. 1968? That means it's not 1960 anymore! Am I back in my hotel room?

I saw a TV cabinet, microwave and mini fridge. The clock on the nightstand said 8:25 a.m. I saw my cell phone on the nightstand and grabbed it to check the date. I clicked on my calendar and saw December 28, 2006. Was it all a dream? But it couldn't be – it lasted for days!

I dropped back down onto the pillow, searching my mind the way I'd done many times after waking from a dream or a nightmare. *Graceland was real! Elvis was real!* All of the feelings and emotions were too powerful to be part of my subconscious.

I swung my legs off the bed and wandered around the room, looking for something. Anything. Proof.

I looked at myself in the bathroom mirror. I was wearing a blue robe with the initials EP monogrammed on the chest. EP... Elvis Presley. Here was the proof! I didn't own this robe before today. Nor these slippers on my feet. And where is the outfit I wore to Beale Street?

I searched the room for the jeans and turtleneck but could

not find them. I leaned against the wall between the bathroom and bedroom. I was cold, so I pulled my Elvis robe tighter around me. Where was Elvis' body heat when I needed it? I looked at the bed. Oh, Elvis, I miss you!

I don't know how many minutes passed but I was startled when my cell phone beeped with an incoming text message. I picked it up and saw the text from Chris: Awake yet? Meet @ continental b'fast, 9 a.m. Elvis is waiting. What did he mean by that? Is Elvis here? I'm so confused!

I sat back down on the bed. I should get in the shower but couldn't find the energy to do anything else but ponder my situation. Had I lost my mind? Was I destined for a mental institution? Slowly, the fog started to lift from my brain and I knew what I had to do. I didn't want to let go of what happened, what I remembered. I grabbed my journal from the desk and sat back down on the bed. I started writing as fast as I could. *Write it down, Maggie. All of it.*

My furious scribbling was interrupted by a knock on the door. I was engrossed in what I was doing, it made me jump. I opened the door to find Chris standing there with two steaming cups of coffee.

"Good morning!" he said enthusiastically. "You're still in your robe! Didn't you get my text? You do know I'm on deadline for this story, right? We've got to hit the road!" He took a step forward to come into the room but I did not move. I just gazed at him in silence. "What's the matter?" he said. "Oh. I'm not allowed in your room. Sorry." He handed me one of the cups of coffee as he took a step backward. "Here, drink this. It will help you wake up." I took a sip. It tasted good. I took a step back as well, opening the door so he could enter. Still, I had not said a word. Chris stepped into the room. "Maggie… is something wrong? I've never seen you this quiet."

I looked at him, met his eyes and said, "I've been there."

"Where?" he asked.

"To Graceland."

"I know. Me, too. Remember our tour together yesterday?"

"No. I mean with *him*."

"Him who?"

"Elvis!"

"Sure, I suppose in some way Elvis is with all who enter his house," he said, cocking his head sideways. He thinks I'm crazy.

I turned away and started crying. I sat down on the bed. Chris rushed to my side, kneeling on the floor in front of me. He took both of our coffees and set them on the nightstand. "Maggie, what's the matter?" He put his hand on my shoulder. "Are you sick? Hung over? Did you have a bad dream?"

I shook my head. "It wasn't a dream. It couldn't have been. It seemed so real."

Now Chris was looking at me and shaking his head. With both hands on my shoulders, he said, "It's OK, Maggie. You're OK." He paused. "How about a hot shower? That will make you feel better. I'll start the water running then hit the lobby with my laptop while you get ready." I nodded but didn't move from the bed.

Chris went to the bathroom and turned on the shower. He came to me again and this time lifted me up from the bed so we were eye to eye. "C'mon, Maggie, we had a great time yesterday and I've got an interesting Elvis story to write. On deadline. Get in the shower and you'll feel like a new person." He kissed me on the forehead and left me alone.

That was just it – I didn't want to feel like a new person. I wanted to go back to Graceland.

The coffee *was* the jolt I needed. I remembered the reason why Chris and I came to Graceland, to write a newspaper story. And I knew he had a tight deadline of later today.

I put myself in robotic mode and went through the motions of a hot shower, hair and makeup, and getting dressed. Along the way, I packed my things. As I carefully folded my Elvis Presley robe, the possible circumstantial proof of my time travel to Graceland, my Elvis sunglasses fell out of the pocket. I put the robe in the duffle bag and the sunglasses in my purse. It didn't strike me as strange until later – that those sunglasses had made their way to the past and back to the present just as I had.

The next time Chris came calling for me, I was ready. "Now that's the Maggie I remember!" he greeted me, stepping in to the room to grab my duffle bag and a few items on hangers. "You look great. Refreshed. Ready for another 300-mile journey." He was quite cheerful.

I couldn't help but smile and say, "Thanks."

We piled our belongings, including my Elvis shopping bags, into his car and went to see what was left of the free continental breakfast. I wasn't very hungry so I grabbed a banana and another coffee. We checked out and left the hotel.

When we made a left on to Elvis Presley Boulevard, Chris eased the car over to the tourist lane in front of Graceland. The gates were open and tour buses were going back and forth. "Time to say goodbye," he said.

"I feel like I shouldn't," I said pensively.

"Say goodbye? Why not?" he asked.

"I need to go back."

"You can always go back, Maggie. Graceland isn't going anywhere. They're making way too much money to shut this place down."

I sighed. "It was so real."

"What was? Oh, your dream about Elvis. Sounds like a good story, Maggie. Have you thought about writing it down? Maybe it's worth sharing."

"Actually, I've already started. After I woke up and was utterly confused, I put some notes in my journal."

"Good. From one writer to another, it's always good to get things down on paper." He hit the steering wheel with both hands. "Ready to hit the road?"

I took a deep breath and exhaled. "Sure. Let's go."

Chris listened to music on Memphis radio. I was lost in thought, going over details in my mind. Did I really travel through time? It seems like the portal to 1960 was in Elvis' storage closet in the basement. That's where I first remember being at Graceland and also my last memory of Graceland. As for how I left 2006, I could only think of the bed in my hotel room. It's the last place I crashed after our night on Beale Street. Did I roll over into a rabbit hole? Oh, I wish I could go back to my room! I should have inspected the bed more. Maybe I would have gone right back to Elvis's storage room and upstairs to his warm bed to snuggle with him while he slept.

"What's on your mind, Maggie?" Chris asked, interrupting my time warp analysis. "Everything OK? Honestly, when you're this quiet, it's a little creepy."

I gave him a look. "I don't mean you're giving me the creeps," he said. "I just like to hear your voice and see you smile."

"I'm sorry." I faked a smile for him. "I know I'm a little off today. It's just…" I looked at him and he glanced at me but returned his eyes to the road. "If I tell you what's on my mind, you'll think I'm crazy."

"Try me. I'm a reporter, remember? I've heard a lot of crazy shit."

I took another deep breath and turned down the radio. "I've been to 1960. December 1960. To Graceland. And Elvis. I met Elvis. He was alive and well, home for Christmas, back from the Army, on break from making movies in Hollywood. I spent a few days and nights with him and his family and friends. It was… incredible. And memorable."

I looked at Chris. He seemed to be thinking of what to say next. "That sounds like a very worthwhile dream."

"I'm not finished. It wasn't a dream, Chris. I…" I paused, barely believing it myself. "I traveled through time. I can prove it! I think. There was some kind of portal or rabbit hole in my hotel room. The bed. When I went to bed after our night on Beale Street, I woke up at Graceland. I was in a storage closet in Elvis' basement!"

Chris started laughing. "Wouldn't it have been more convenient if the Graceland portal was Elvis' bed?" He saw that I was not laughing at all. "I'm sorry, Maggie. But I think you just had an amazing dream about Elvis. He's always on your mind. You've talked about him nearly the whole time we've been together. It makes perfect sense that you would dream about him, too."

"I knew you wouldn't believe me," I said defensively.

"I want to believe you. Time travel would be the story of the century! I'd love to have the inside scoop on that." He winked at me when he said this.

I was still all business. "Do you remember what I wore to Beale Street the other night?"

"Uh… clothes? No. I'm a guy, I don't remember things like

that."

"I wore jeans and a turtleneck, Chris. And that's what I was wearing in December 1960 in Graceland. Elvis' cousin Patsy helped me freshen up and dress up because she said I looked too casual to meet Elvis." I paused. "When I woke up this morning in 2006, I was wearing an Elvis Presley monogrammed robe and slippers. I never owned those items before! And... my jeans and turtleneck were nowhere to be found in my room."

"Maybe I took them off of you," Chris joked. "You had pretty much to drink, remember?"

"Stop trying to be funny, Chris! I'm serious!"

"My apologies. You've given me a lot to think about. I need a few minutes to digest this information." He turned up the radio and focused on the road.

I glared at him. "Don't you dare patronize me."

We were quiet. I was beginning to wonder if I had lost my mind. My head hurt. The day was super bright.

I reached into my purse for my sunglasses. I opened them to put them on and noticed a piece of paper sticking out of the arm. I looked closer. The paper was rolled up and woven in and out of a few of the cut-out circles in the arm of the glasses. I wiggled it loose. Chris glanced at me and asked, "One of those difficult-to-remove price tags?"

I kept working on the paper. Soon I had it free and began unrolling it. It was some kind of newsprint. There was writing on it. When I unrolled it all the way, I gasped. "Oh my God!" I put my hand over my mouth as I read the lines of handwritten words:

M – *isses her mama like I miss mine*
O – *pinions (O be quiet!)*

O – oh so sexy
D – imples (also Different)
Y – ou're a stranger but you can see inside me
I can't figure her out but I like MOODY anyway,
Elvis

"Maggie! What's the matter? What does it say?" Chris questioned.

"It's a note. From Elvis!?" I read the words to Chris, the emotion very palpable in my voice.

"Let me see that."

I handed the note to him. "Be careful."

Chris read the words himself. "Who's Moody?"

"That was Elvis' nickname for me."

Chris looked at me like I was crazy for sure, then back to the note. He said, "Holy shit. Look at the bottom of the note." He handed the note back to me. There were some printed words. They read: *The Commercial Appeal*, December 29, 1960. Holy shit is right.

"This is real! This is proof that I was with Elvis! He was reading the paper in bed one night. My sunglasses were on the nightstand because he thought they were strange and tried them on and I told him he was a trendsetter. He must have torn off a page of the newspaper and wrote me a note. You have to believe me now, Chris! This is proof!"

"Did you have sex with Elvis Presley?" he asked.

"Sex? Why are you thinking about sex at a time like this? This is huge! Let's turn around and go back! We have to get back into my hotel room and see if we can go back to 1960 Graceland. I didn't get to say goodbye to Elvis. I didn't get to tell him…"

Chris interrupted me. "Calm down, Maggie. Relax. I admit, you've got quite a story. This note on a piece of 1960 newspaper is freaky shit worth investigating. But I have to get back to St. Louis and file my story today, the story we went to Memphis to write, or my editor will be all over my ass. Now… I'm not saying that you shouldn't go back to Memphis. Maybe I'll even tag along if you'll let me. But first I think you should get out a pen and paper and *write*. Write down everything you can remember, Maggie, about what happened. Or didn't happen."

I gave him a dirty look. "It happened, Chris."

I reached into my bag in the back seat and pulled out my journal. I put it on my lap and stared out the front window.

Could I really go back and see Elvis again? I wonder what he thought when he woke up and discovered I was gone. Did he miss me? He has so many women and he's in love with Priscilla, the girl he will marry. Plus, there's Anita, whom he had a date with for New Year's Eve, so I'd be a fool to think he would give me a second thought. And yet… there was the note. To Moody from Elvis. I tucked it safely inside my journal. And returned to my thoughts.

Chris looked at me. "You said it happened."

"Yes it did," I said emphatically.

"You had sex with Elvis Presley."

"Chris, I swear you have a one track mind!"

"I'm sorry but that's major news. Sex with the King of Rock 'n Roll. That's a killer story. You better write it down, Maggie. Every last detail."

"Pervert."

"Nope. Just jealous."

I looked at him with raised eyebrows. "Jealous of Elvis? Wow."

"Jealous of Elvis with *you*." He winked again and held up his hand for a high five. "Friends?" he said. I high fived him and our fingers entwined. We kept them like that and lowered them to rest them on the console. More than friends? Maybe.

"Since I've got hold of your writing hand, do you think you can play one-arm DJ until we hit the KSHE 95 airwaves? I don't even mind if you want to play Elvis music but as soon as 94.7 FM tunes in, we're going to listen to real rock."

"Elvis is the reason for your real rock," I said as I nudged my elbow into his side.

I obliged. I knew just the song. It came to me like a whisper from the past. I plugged my iPod into Chris's car stereo and scrolled through my playlists until I found what I wanted to hear. I sat back, still holding hands with this reporter-turned-friend-turned-who-knows-what and listened to Elvis sing:

Well, it's hard to be a gambler betting on a number
that changes every time
When you think you're gonna win, you think she's giving in,
a stranger's all you find
Yeah, it's hard to figure out what she's all about
but she's woman through and through
She's a complicated lady, so color my baby – Moody Blue.

Oh, Moody Blue, tell me am I getting through
I keep hanging on trying to learn your song but I never do
Oh, Moody Blue, tell me who I'm talking to
You're like night and day, it's hard to say which one is you ...

As I listened to the rest of the song that had new meaning for me now, my thoughts returned to the days and nights I spent with Elvis Presley. I miss him. I want to see him again. I didn't get to say goodbye. I didn't get to tell him to take better care of himself.

I looked down at the hand that was holding mine, giving me new present-day hope. I watched the highway mile markers count the growing distance from Graceland. Amid all of the uncertainty, I was sure of one thing: I have to go back.

The End

ACKNOWLEDGEMENTS

OVER THE RAINBOW (from "The Wizard of Oz")
Music by HAROLD ARLEN
Lyrics by E.Y. HARBURG
©1938 (Renewed) METRO-GOLDWYN-MAYER INC.
©1939 (Renewed) EMI FEIST CATALOG INC.
All Rights Controlled and Administered by EMI FEIST
CATALOG INC. (Publishing) and ALFRED MUSIC (Print)
All Rights Reserved.

MOODY BLUE
Written by Mark James
©1975 Screen Gems-EMI Music Inc.
All rights administered by Sony/ATV Music Publishing LLC.
424 Church Street, Suite 1200, Nashville, TN 37219.
All rights reserved. Used by permission.

AUTHOR'S NOTE

It's a blessing, not only to be a writer but to be one with cheerleaders. Throughout this process, I've had many family, friends and colleagues express enthusiasm, provide encouragement and quite possibly, feign interest in EP. They deserve my wholehearted thanks.

To Joyce Romine, who was the first to read *Waking up in Graceland*, thanks for your thoughtful corrections, edits and suggestions. I believe this book is better because of you.

To my advance readers, who lent their feedback as well:

Kati Eddinger, my beloved sister and friend. You read more books than anyone I know (except Dad). You work in the publishing world. I could not wait to hear what you thought of my book.

Chris Scherting, my best friend from high school. We've been through a lot and shared even more. You say you're a Kelly Peach fan, well, I'm a Chris Scherting fan!

Cindy Denner, my best friend from the Florida years and an inspiring teacher of today's youth. I miss you terribly but know that our hearts are connected because we jump right back into our friendship every time we reunite.

Becky Reichardt, one of the smartest people I know and my "pinafore" pal. Through kinship, we've learned that what happens behind the scenes is always more interesting. I think we should give some serious thought to that book we want to write together.

Katie Robinson, my colleague and friend. I'm glad we met through work and found many laughs amidst the versions, revisions and deadlines. Thanks also for your alluring design of my book cover.

To my amazing parents, George Peach and Mary Reese, and stepparents, Marie McGlynn-Peach and Bob Reese, thanks for your unconditional love and support. You molded me into who I am and I'm twice blessed with parental friendship and guidance.

To my brother and sister, Gary Peach and Becky Garozzo, I share this with you and hope you find a few hidden gems inside from our years together at 6950.

To my extended family, including cousins, nieces, nephews and steps, you are my celebration. Thanks for giving me a full and blessed life.

To my closest friends, it's my goal to make you laugh yet you are the ones who make me smile: Debbie Costrino, Cindy Koehler, Carla Russell, Jim McMullan, Sheri Naumann, Mary Pat Admire, Jill Bollwerk, Lisa Bozdeck, Chris Cordes, Warren Laird, Jen Borgra, Diana Reed, Louisa Dean, Carol Owens, Jenny Parmentier, Nicole Harvey, Armando Hernandez, Erin Jones, Audra, Mini and Kiki Laird, Alex, Geni and Mark Metzger, Julie Lally, Cheryl Cavins, Stephanie Perry, Stephanie Nigh and Karen Kelly.

Thanks to the professionals who helped me publish this book: Ed Moore, Frank Janoski and Laura Jones. When I needed an accountant, a lawyer and a printer, you were there with expert advice and opinions.

To Priscilla and Lisa Marie Presley, thanks for all you've done to share Elvis with the rest of the world. You could have kept him to yourselves, but instead poured your hearts into efforts to keep his legacy and light alive for generations to come.

To my Friends in Elvis, including all of you hunka hunka

Elvis Tribute Artists, no one on the outside looking in can quite understand how much we love the King. It's been great fun sharing Elvis experiences with you. Let's keep 'em coming.

BIBLIOGRAPHY

These books helped my research for this novel:

Cocke, Marian J.
I Called Him Babe, 1979.

Klein, George with Chuck Crisafulli.
Elvis: My Best Man, 2010.

Mason, Bobbie Ann.
Elvis Presley, 2003.

McKeon, Elizabeth and Linda Everett.
Elvis Speaks, 1997, 2004.

Nichopoulos, George, M.D. with Rose Clayton Phillips.
The King and Dr. Nick, 2009.

Presley, Priscilla Beaulieu with Sandra Harmon.
Elvis and Me, 1985.

Rooks, Nancy with Jim Cox.
Inside Graceland, 2005.

Schilling, Jerry with Chuck Crisafulli.
Me and a Guy Named Elvis, 2006.

West, Sonny with Marshall Terrill.
Elvis: Still Taking Care of Business, 2007.